Miltiades turned a[...]
It's long past time t[...]
truth, doppleganger."

"How charming," Eidola hissed. As Miltiades advanced on her, she suddenly pressed her fist into her midsection, just beneath her heart. Eyes dripping venom, she reached inside her own torso and removed a single white gemstone, holding it clenched in her hand. "Enough of this. Do any of you recognize what I hold in my hand?"

FORGOTTEN REALMS
Fantasy Adventure

The DOUBLE DIAMOND TRIANGLE SAGA™

THE ABDUCTION
J. Robert King

THE PALADINS
James M. Ward & David Wise

THE MERCENARIES
Ed Greenwood

ERRAND OF MERCY
Roger E. Moore

AN OPPORTUNITY FOR PROFIT
Dave Gross

CONSPIRACY
J. Robert King

UNEASY ALLIANCES
David Cook with Peter Archer

EASY BETRAYALS
Richard Baker

THE DIAMOND
J. Robert King & Ed Greenwood

FORGOTTEN REALMS®
Fantasy Adventure

The DOUBLE DIAMOND TRIANGLE SAGA™

Part 8

EASY BETRAYALS

Richard Baker

EASY BETRAYALS

©1998 TSR, Inc.

All Rights Reserved.

All characters in this book are fictitious. Any resemblance to actual persons, living or dead, is purely coincidental.

This book is protected under the copyright laws of the United States of America. Any reproduction or unauthorized use of the material or artwork contained herein is prohibited without the express written permission of TSR, Inc.

Distributed to the book trade in the United States by Random House, Inc. and in Canada by Random House of Canada, Ltd.

Distributed to the hobby, toy, and comic trade in the United States and Canada by regional distributors.

Distributed worldwide by Wizards of the Coast, Inc. and regional distributors.

FORGOTTEN REALMS and the TSR logo are registered trademarks owned by TSR, Inc. DOUBLE DIAMOND TRIANGLE SAGA is a trademark owned by TSR, Inc.

All TSR characters, character names, and the distinctive likenesses thereof are trademarks owned by TSR, Inc.

TSR, Inc., a subsidiary of Wizards of the Coast, Inc.
All rights reserved. Made in the U.S.A.

Cover art by Heather LeMay
First Printing: June 1998
Library of Congress Catalog Card Number: 96-90571

9 8 7 6 5 4 3 2 1

ISBN: 0-7869-0871-8
8641XXX1501

U.S., CANADA, ASIA,	EUROPEAN HEADQUARTERS
PACIFIC, & LATIN AMERICA	Wizards of the Coast, Belgium
Wizards of the Coast, Inc.	P.B. 34
P.O. Box 707	2300 Turnhout
Renton, WA 98057-0707	Belgium
+1-206-624-0933	+32-14-44-30-44

Visit our website at **www.tsr.com**

Prelude
The best-laid plans . . .

Killing the human boy was a mistake.

I could have used him if I'd only managed to contain my rage. Quick and remorseless action in direct pursuit of a goal is one thing, but murder for the joy of it . . . I usually demand more of myself. Months of entrapment in Eidola's shape—worse yet, entrapment in Eidola's *persona*—have left me bereft of patience and subtlety.

Damn those interfering wizards! What sorcery did they use to pierce my disguise? If they hadn't bound me with that cursed girdle, I could have eluded Aetheric's magical warriors with ease. I'd be in Waterdeep, Piergeiron safely in my hands. . . not standing in some forsaken dungeon in the Utter East, thousands of miles from my mission.

But . . .

It's still not out of reach. I don't know what moved Piergeiron to send that stupid boy—was Noph his name?—to my rescue. Who else could I have duped into removing the girdle? I didn't lie outright when I told the boy the magical girdle prevented my escape from Aetheric's mundane shackles; I just neglected to tell him *who* had bound me and exactly *how* it interfered with my freedom of movement. You have to use your wits to weave a lie that isn't a lie, after all.

When Noph removed the accursed girdle, he unwittingly freed me to do anything I want, to *be* anyone I can imagine. And how'd I thank him? In a moment of weakness I reveled in freedom with a wasteful and stupid act of violence. Better by far to have endured my imprisonment in Eidola a few hours more and *allowed* myself to be rescued. And yet . . . what if I was the victim of someone else's deception? The Blackstaff must be involved in this, and he knows me too well.

I shed the mastiff with ease and stand for a rare instant in my natural shape. I've been so many others for so long, I've almost forgotten who I am. Where now? Filthy water laps and swirls in the hallway, draining down the stone stairs to the level of my former cell. Steel clashes, monstrous things scream and howl, and magic thunders in the chambers below. What was it Noph said? Piergeiron sent *him* to rescue me. That I doubt. The armored warriors and fierce rogues I fled from below probably comprised the real rescue party.

And what of this lasso? Somehow, that cursed boy found the strength to hurl a snare after me when I left him torn and dying. Have I exchanged one magical bond for another?

I'll not be bound again! I fashion talons of steel with a moment's thought, but the hempen coil resists my claws. I grow the bulging thews of a minotaur, and I cannot burst it. I shift to the boneless grace of an octopus, yet still it circles me. The lariat has me well and truly caught. Damn that wretched boy! Maybe I don't regret killing him after all.

My natural form won't do. I'll need some cloak before I leave this place . . . . Eidola will serve. Noph's companions can't know that he saw me change. Rippling with the effort of the crafting , I create a high-collared leather jacket to hide the rope around my neck and coil the remaining line into my coat. Straight and tall, a broad-shouldered warrioress with smooth muscles and a face of heart-wrenching beauty . . . I've plenty of ploys I can try with this form. Tight-fitting leather pants and a corselet of shining mail complete the disguise. My right hand is empty. With a thought I grow a long, straight sword blade from my palm and craft an empty scabbard by my left hip at the same time.

With the girdle gone, I'm in a better position to finish my mission from a dungeon in the Utter East than I was in when I stood at Piergeiron's side in Waterdeep. Aetheric's interference has provided an opportunity I never could have created under the watchful eyes of Khelben and the other Waterdhavians.

If I can only make my way back to Waterdeep, all will still be well.

Armored men, clattering and bounding up the steps below. They pursue me?

What did the Blackstaff tell them?

If I'd spared the boy, I could have extracted what I need from him. Then I'd know if the men below are here to rescue me, or to make sure that I never return to Waterdeep.

Killing Noph was a mistake.

Chapter 1
Pursuit

Battered and exhausted, Belgin sprinted after the warriors of Tyr, splashing through the cold water that swirled and surged in the dim hallway. He caught one brief glimpse of a dark beast bounding up the stairs at the end of the corridor, trailing a cord, and then the creature darted out of sight in the stone labyrinth of Aetheric's dungeons. "Rings, Belgin, go after the doppelganger. Join the damned paladins if you must, but make sure one of you slays her. We want our reward."

Entreri didn't waste words, reflected Belgin. Fine. He'd follow the assassin's orders and be done with the whole affair. No mere chest of jewels could possibly compensate him for the pain and madness he'd already endured, and every moment he delayed in the execution of Entreri's command only added to his losses.

He wheezed and gasped for breath as he floundered after Miltiades and Jacob. Water dragged at his tailored trousers and waistcoat, and a dozen bruises and sprains announced themselves as he drove forward. "Come on, Rings," he huffed. The effort of speaking as he ran brought on a fit of coughing that raked his chest with fiery knives. Bright flecks of blood staining his beard, Belgin ignored his distress and staggered on. He'd had plenty of practice of late.

Behind him, the dwarven pirate known as Rings struggled valiantly to keep up with his human companions. The icy water stood chest-high on the dwarf, and he flailed and spluttered as he trailed Belgin. "Don't wait on me," the dwarf growled. "You keep the paladins in sight. I'll catch up!"

"Not this time," Belgin answered. He slowed and caught the dwarf's arm, towing him along. "If I object to anything that those two"—he nodded at the Tyrian warriors—"decide to do, I want you nearby to help argue my point." Ahead of them, Miltiades reached the stairs at the end of the hall and clambered out of the water, his long shanks working like pistons as he propelled himself up the steps. Jacob followed a moment later, brandishing his two-handed sword like a promise of justice. *They've spent the day fighting an untold number of fiends,* Belgin thought enviously, *and still they're fresh enough to sprint up stairs wearing armor from head to toe.*

Winded and shivering with cold, the moon-faced sharper took the steps as fast as he could, Rings following. "Why'd we . . . whew! . . . have to go chasing after . . . the doppelganger?" the dwarf complained. "I'm not made for . . . chasing down long-legged humans! If Entreri wanted her dead . . . he could have bloody well done it himself."

"He's got another game . . . to play . . . I think," the sharper answered, puffing for breath. They reached a long, torchlit corridor at the top of the stairs. The two paladins still ran on ahead, mail and plate clattering like an engine made of kitchenware. Belgin paused for breath, leaning forward with his hands on his knees. "He was . . . very interested . . . in the bloodforge, you'll recall."

"Damn!" Rings scowled. "Now we're out of his way. He can go get it without worrying about the two of us."

Belgin bit his lip, thinking of the assassin's inhuman speed and the cold, flat determination behind his eyes. "He wasn't worried about us anyway, Rings."

The dwarf glanced up to meet his eyes. Brass rings piercing his eyebrows glinted in the torchlight. "So what are we doing here? I've no need to meddle in the affairs of wizards and fiends. We can walk back down those stairs, collect Sharessa and Ingrar, and cut our losses now."

"I'm not ready to cross Entreri yet. Maybe not ever," Belgin said slowly. "Even if I didn't think that he'd kill us in the blink of an eye for turning on him, I signed a contract to kill Eidola, whoever or whatever she turned out to be. We all did. I'm going to live up to my word at least this once. If we walk out of this now, then it's all for nothing. Anvil, Kurthe, Brindra—they're dead for no reason at all, and I can't live with that."

Rings held his gaze a moment more, then nodded abruptly. "You talk too much, Belgin, but you're right. Come on—they're getting away from us." Fighting axe in one gnarled fist, the dwarven pirate loped down the passageway. Belgin straightened and ran after him. The hallway terminated in a series of twisting stairs and narrow guard chambers. They sprinted through mossy stone doorways and pelted across crooked arcades, the warriors ahead of them flitting in and out of the shadows like bright coins spinning down into a dark well.

In moments, Belgin lost all sense of direction. The paladins dashed from one room to the next as if they feared nothing, leaping headlong into each turn and twist of the chase. Consumed by their righteous rage, they had no thought for caution or subtlety, only justice.

Once Belgin saw Jacob turn his head to fix one eye on the following rogues, but then the noble warrior returned his attention to the chase. He thinks we don't matter, Belgin realized. He narrowed his eyes and redoubled his efforts.

Abruptly, the chase ended. Belgin turned a corner and found the paladin and the swordsman halted in front of him, facing a vast open gallery. They stood on a precarious balcony, glaring out at the nighted space ahead. Rings barreled into the sharper from behind, almost knocking him flat. Belgin staggered and went to one knee.

"What? What is it?" Rings barked, crouching in the entranceway.

"Trouble," answered Jacob. Belgin followed his eyes and gasped in horror. On the opposite balcony, a stone's throw away, stood a creature of nightmare. Tall as an ogre, with scaly skin and a barbed tail that twitched and slashed the air around it, its great leathery wings draped its shoulders like a cloak of despair. A whip of fire dangled from one clawed hand. The creature turned to a shadowed vulturelike shape at its side and pointed toward the paladins. "Slay them," it grated in a voice of stone. The vulture-thing launched itself into the air with a disheveled flurry of shabby, stinking feathers, joined a moment later by two more of its kind that dropped from the black recesses above.

" 'Ware the vrock!" shouted Miltiades, raising his hammer. The first of the fiends descended on him with clashing beak and grasping talons, crushing him to the ground. The paladin's hammer rose and fell, then rose again with dark gore wreathing its silver head. The vrock's companion stooped on Jacob, only to be driven back by the white razor of the warrior's flashing sword.

The third soared over the fighters in the front and dove at Belgin. "Another fiend. Great," he managed weakly, raising his cutlass in feeble protest. He slashed blindly as a storm of talon and and claw descended on him, ripping through the fancy leather jerkin to rake deep, foul furrows in the flesh beneath. Belgin screamed in pain and fear, ramming the point of his cutlass into the center of the vrock's chest.

The blade slid in without a mark. Belgin wrenched it free, but the vrock only laughed, its voice clashing like cymbals of brass. "Mundane steel holds no power over one of my kind, mortal," it hissed in delight. "You'll need a better weapon than that to draw my blood."

"How about this one?" From the creature's flank, Rings struck out with his wicked axe, shearing through its scabrous wing. Belgin gagged in disgust as the creature's black blood drenched and seared him. The dwarf hacked brutally at the fiend as it scrabbled away from him. "No one's ever called the steel of my fathers' axe mundane!" the dwarf shouted fiercely. "Take some of this back to the Abyss with you!"

Belgin regained his feet. In the corner of his eye he saw Miltiades standing, shouldering aside the corpse of the vrock that had assailed him, while Jacob slashed his foe to pieces with his great blade. At the edge of the balcony, the third vrock wheeled and lashed out with its talons, smashing Rings to the ground. With one quick step the sharper leaped into the air and planted his feet in the center of the fiend's torso, catapulting it from the stone shelf. The fiend shrieked horribly, trying to hold the air with its ruined pinions, and spiraled out of sight into the darkness below. Picking himself up, Belgin looked around for the next foe.

"Forget the vrock! 'Ware the balor!" Jacob shouted, holding his blade on guard against the fiery titan that stood on the opposite side of the hall.

For one tense moment, both paladins and pirates stood together, waiting for the powerful fiend to attack. It glared at them, its eyes burning. Then, in a motion so smooth and effortless it seemed impossible, it shrank and darkened into the form of a leather-clad human woman. Her teeth bared in a sharklike grin, Eidola laughed at them. "Not bad," she remarked. "I see that Piergeiron didn't waste his time with amateurs, excepting that boy Noph, anyway."

"Hold there!" shouted Miltiades, brandishing his

hammer. "You've much to answer for, monster! Surrender now, and you'll live to see a fair trial in Tyr's hall."

"Forgive me if I decline," the woman sneered. "I have places to go, paladin, and I think I'll find my own way. Do yourself a favor and find some other damsel in distress to rescue."

"I came halfway across the world to punish those who stole you," the paladin grated. "Now your own lies have damned you. I don't care how many secret allies you have here or what kind of deceptions you've created to deter me from my mission, monster—you've leagued yourself with the wrong patrons." He paced forward to the edge of the balcony, eyeing the jump. "I'll bring Tyr's justice to you or die trying."

"Now I remember why I detest paladins," Eidola remarked. She turned to leave.

Moved by a flicker of intuition, Belgin stepped forward. "Eidola!" he cried. "Where are you going?"

"I don't know," she replied instantly. "I mean to find my way back to Waterdeep as quickly as possible, but I don't know where I am." Her face suddenly contorted in anger, and she reached up with one hand to tug at her collar. "What in the name of darkness?" she muttered. White hemp showed around the hollow of her throat.

Belgin grinned. He'd guessed right—Noph's magical lasso retained its power to compel its victim to truthfulness, even though no one held the doppelganger captive. "Why did Aetheric imprison you? You were doing his work, weren't you?"

On the opposite balcony, the woman gasped and fell to her knees, struggling with all her will to keep from answering. It wasn't enough. "He kidnapped me because he believed I was exactly what I pretended to be," she rasped. "Garkim said that Aetheric stole me to provoke Piergeiron into sending a rescue party. He hoped to turn you against the fiends who beset Doegan, since the bloodforge had sapped the strength from his own people."

"Belgin? What's going on?" demanded Jacob. The powerful warrior turned a glare of black suspicion on him, sword raised belligerently.

Rings moved to intercede, but Miltiades answered for him. "Noph's lasso," he said. "She's caught in it and can't lie to us." He looked back to Eidola. "What were you doing in Waterdeep? What evil ensorcellment did you work against Piergeiron, creature?"

The doppleganger's mouth opened, but in the blink of an eye she seemed to twist and shift. The great black mastiff stood in her place. It growled and fixed one last venomous glance on the battered adventurers, then turned and bounded into the dark passage behind her.

"Eidola!" howled Miltiades. "There is no place in this world distant enough, dark enough, foul enough to hide you from Tyr's justice! Answer me!"

"Forget it, paladin," said Rings. "She's gone. You might be able to make her speak truth, but if she chooses a form incapable of speech you can't compel her to obey you."

"I'm not done with her yet," Miltiades snapped. He stepped to the edge of the balcony, then the sides, studying the great gallery. "Come on. I think we can cross farther down."

"She can be anything she wants," Jacob said. "We might never catch her. Shouldn't we go after Entreri instead to make sure the bloodforge is destroyed? We've a better chance at that."

Miltiades shook his head. "You heard her. She means to return to Waterdeep and finish whatever plot she started there. Someone's got to stop her."

"We're in the Utter East, Miltiades. It'd take her months to get back to Waterdeep."

"It might take us months, too." The tall paladin closed his eyes, thinking or praying, and then opened them again. "We follow the doppelganger, Jacob. I fear for Kern and Trandon, too, but I feel that Tyr means us to take this path."

Jacob opened his mouth as if to argue the point further, but surrendered. "Okay. We'll run her to ground, if we can. Now, what of these two?" He indicated Belgin and Rings with a jerk of his thumb.

Belgin watched the two warriors warily. He felt Rings shift behind him, moving closer for support. "You've known our intentions toward the lady all along," the sharper said. "You call it justice, we call it business, but we mean to see her dead. We gave our word on it."

"What's that worth?" Jacob said icily.

Belgin put out a hand to steady Rings as the dwarf stepped up, eyes blazing. "This day, as much as yours," he said. "We've got a better reason to cooperate now than we did before. If that's not good enough for you, Rings and I will go our own way. But we'll be following the doppelganger, I promise you."

Jacob's eyes narrowed, but he slowly relented, a shallow smile on his face. I know that look, Belgin mused. That's the look that says, I could kill you now, but I'd rather kill you later. Meeting the fighter's sneer with a smirk of his own, Belgin bowed formally. "If we're agreed, then, let's get to it," he said. "We've a shapeshifter to catch."

* * * * *

They scrambled down several levels, scaling the stone balustrades that ringed the gallery's upper corridors, then crossed on a narrow buttress of stone that bridged the dark hall. On the opposite side, they cautiously clambered up the ancient facade and set off down the hallway into which Eidola had disappeared. It was a dirty, strenuous exercise that left Belgin's limbs quivering with strain and a deep, burring rasp in his chest, but he found the strength to make the crossing without calling on his companions for aid.

"She's got a half-hour lead on us, at least," Jacob grumbled. "How can you catch something that can grow wings, or fins, or extra legs anytime she feels like it?"

"Perseverance," Miltiades replied. Drawn and haggard, bloodied by a dozen small wounds, it seemed that nothing but determination kept the paladin on his feet. "She'll give up before we will."

"Pray we catch up to her before she finds her way out of these crypts," said Belgin. "If she gets to the city above, perseverance won't matter."

"We'll see." Miltiades shrugged sparely and returned his attention to the hall before them. The dismal sconces of the mage-king's dungeons were far behind them, and with a muttered prayer the paladin halted to conjure a shining white light on the head of his warhammer, illuminating the corridor. It was long and straight, faced with a faded and peeling plaster that bore hints of ancient murals. Dust lay thick on the floor, but scuffling paw prints showed where Eidola had passed.

With a silent exchange of glances, the four men pressed farther into the crypt. Belgin coughed in the musty air, holding a handkerchief to his face. "What kind of maze is this place?" he muttered into the darkness.

"Old work, old human work," Rings replied softly. The dwarf ran his gnarled hand along the rotten plaster of the wall. "It's not the same construction as the rest of Aetheric's halls."

"Ancient Mar stonework?"

"It might be. It looks like the Mar ruins I've seen scattered around the Five Kingdoms." The dwarf tugged on an earring. "This feels like a funeral chamber of some kind."

"Great. A crypt," Jacob remarked over his shoulder.

"If you're right, Rings, we might not have a long chase on our hands after all," Belgin said thoughtfully. "Eidola might have fled into a dead end—er, so to speak."

They traveled several hundred yards before the passageway ended in a great double door of stone. One valve stood ajar. Belgin knelt by the floor, examining the tracks. The four-footed paw marks had vanished, replaced by the slim outline of a woman's boots. "She took human form again here," he advised the others, rising and dusting his hands against his trousers.

"You seem to have a knack for reading tracks," Jacob observed. "I thought you were a sea dog, not a highwayman."

"I've a few tricks up my sleeve," the sharper answered. Miltiades moved up, turned his broad shoulders sideways, and slipped into the chamber beyond. Jacob followed, then Rings. Belgin paused a moment, studying the towering door. He was fairly certain he couldn't have moved it an inch. If you cross swords with her, Belgin my lad, remember that she's much stronger than she looks, he told himself. He straightened his tailored jacket and wriggled past the rough stone, shielding his eyes against the glare of the paladin's magical light.

The room beyond was magnificent, flanked by great statues of ancient warriors in long headdresses. A series of false arches carved in bas-relief along the walls flanked the room, which was cluttered with mildewed banners, broken urns stained with redolent residue, old bronze weapons green with verdigris, and dozens of small casks and statuaries. In the center of the room stood a long, low pedestal supporting a stone sarcophagus, elaborately carved in the likeness of a handsome young man. Dust lay thick over the entire chamber.

Belgin searched the room with his eyes, alert for any threat or sign of Eidola's path. There was no other exit from the chamber.

"We have her," Miltiades said quietly. "Jacob, guard the door. Let nothing pass." The curly-haired fighter scowled at the paladin's order, but he grimaced and took up a watchful post by the door, sword poised like a toll pike. With the patience of a stalking cat, Miltiades advanced into the room, his eyes flicking from place to place as he searched. He circled to the left of the sarcophagus.

Rings watched Miltiades for a moment, then circled around the pedestal to the right, his short axe hanging from his fingertips. Belgin trailed Rings, choosing to cover his friend's back. He'd seen Miltiades fight, and besides, the Sharkers had to watch out for each other more now than ever. The room fell silent, the quiet broken only by the slow scuffle of leather on stone and the soft jingling of the paladin's mail and plate. Nervous sweat trickled down the pirate's brow as the hunt lengthened. "Careful, Rings," he whispered. "She might have changed her form again."

"Could she be a piece of furniture?" the dwarf asked over his shoulder. "A big vase, or maybe a wall hanging?"

"I've heard it said that doppelgangers are limited in how much they can change their shape. Look for something more or less human-sized . . . but don't turn your back on anything."

"That doesn't help," Rings growled in reply. "Belgin, you—"

"Silence, both of you!" barked Miltiades. Belgin shot a resentful glare at the paladin, but Miltiades wasn't looking at the pirates; he stood before a tall funereal statue. It was the image of an ancient warrior much like the others that stood guard over the sarcophagus, with a broad bare chest, a knee-length kilt, sandals, and a high headdress framing its stern face. Its hands gripped an oblong shield and a curving sword. "How many of these stone warriors stand against your wall, Rings?" asked Miltiades, his eyes narrowed in suspicion.

"Seven," the dwarf answered.

"There are eight over here," Miltiades said. He raised his hammer to shatter the image before him.

With preternatural swiftness the stone warrior sprang from its pedestal, lashing out with its heavy blade. Miltiades caught the blow on his shield with a great ringing parry and was driven backward. With mechanical ruthlessness Eidola hammered at the paladin's guard. Rings dashed forward, rounding the central sarcophagus to come to Miltiades's aid. In the corner of his eye, Belgin saw Jacob take three steps from his post by the door, moving up to join the fight. "No, Jacob!" he barked. "Guard the door! We can't let her out of this room!"

The fighter paused, meeting Belgin's face with contemptuous anger. "Then *help* him!" he roared, pointing at the fight. Miltiades slipped and went down to one knee. Eidola screeched in triumph and raised her stone blade to strike—but the paladin shattered one knee with a low swing of his silver hammer. Eidola toppled to the floor just as Rings appeared. The dwarf seized one brawny arm in his left hand and hacked viciously with his axe, breaching the doppelganger's stony hide in a spray of dark blood and flakes of rock-like flesh. Eidola shrieked and convulsed with startling power, hurling the dwarf aside and slamming Miltiades to the floor.

Now! Belgin saw his chance. Nimbly he leaped to the top of the sarcophagus, lashing out with his cutlass to gouge a deep cut across Eidola's forehead as she struggled to stand. The doppelganger fell back, then changed her shape, collapsing into a boneless cuttlefish with razor-sharp hooks serrating its flailing tentacles. Miltiades floundered under the serpentlike strikes of three of the creature's tentacles, then Rings had his axe wrenched from his hand by another. Light and shadow danced chaotically in the tomb as the paladin's glowing hammer whirled and fell. Atop the tomb, Belgin tried to find a place to strike—and then he felt a cold, strong pressure circle his ankle. He stooped to sever the tentacle that gripped his foot, but with inhuman strength Eidola jerked his limb from beneath him, tripping him heavily on top of the sepulchre. The sharper struck his head on the stone face. His eyes flooded with white, and the screaming, clattering, hissing cacophony of the fight faded into nothingness in his ear.

Vision swimming with pain, Belgin at first didn't believe his senses when he felt the stone slab under him begin to grow warm. He rolled to one elbow, trying to regain his bearings, although his movements seemed slow and heavy. Rings and Miltiades still fought Eidola, while Jacob had moved up behind the dwarf, sword raised as he awaited his opportunity to join the fray.

Something black and spidery flitted before Belgin's face. He glanced down in surprise, only to find that glowing magical runes now circled the sarcophagus lid. Above and behind him, the blank wall that stood opposite the chamber's only door seemed to grow a tracery of mystical runes, like ivy climbing a stone wall in the space of only heartbeats. Some kind of enchantment on the sarcophagus? Belgin wondered absently. A tomb-trap triggered by our fighting, or when I fell on the lid? His alertness returning, he rolled off the sepulchre and recovered his sword. "Something's happening!" he called out, warning his companions.

Above the sounds of the fighting, a powerful voice pronounced some horrible doom in a language older than mankind. The great stone door at the tomb's entrance slammed shut with a tremendous boom, bringing a soft rain of dust from the ceiling overhead. Jacob whirled and attacked the doors with all his strength, but they were sealed with sorcery. "We're trapped!" the fighter called.

"Finish the doppelganger!" Miltiades answered, crushing a tentacle to red pulp with one blow of his hammer. "We'll worry about escape once she's dead! For Tyr and justice!" He resumed the attack, striking blow after blow with his hammer while Rings ripped great slashes in the thing with his ancestors' axe. Pieces of cuttlefish lay strewn about the chamber, but still the beast fought on, warping its shape from moment to moment to create new limbs and minimize the effect of its foes' weapons.

Belgin moved in to join the fight again as Jacob did the same, but at that moment the glyphs on the far wall—now an arcane, circular design—flashed with a crackle of energy and a peal of thunder. Where a blank stone wall had stood, a dark portal yawned. Wind howled forth, thick with the scent of dust and strange incense. *What in the Five Kingdoms?* he thought, raising an arm to shield his eyes. *A magical doorway? Here?* "Look out! We might have company coming!"

Eidola recognized the archway, too. Slithering away from the paladin, she seemed to suddenly contract and rise, standing on two legs as the human woman they'd seen before. Deftly she vaulted the stone tomb, parrying Belgin's attack, and leaped headlong into the portal. Belgin dove for the lasso trailing her waist, but the cord brushed his fingertips and disappeared into the darkness. "She's getting away!" he cried unnecessarily.

"Tyr damn it! We had her!" Miltiades shouted. "Quick, after her!"

"Wait!" Jacob shouted against the roaring wind. "We don't know where the portal leads!"

"Jacob's right," Belgin said. "What if it leads to the heart of a volcano? Or to a dragon's den? She might be dead already."

"Then I'm going to go *make sure*," Miltiades stated. Blood streamed from a vicious cut on the side of his head, but the paladin seemed tireless. He took three running steps and threw himself into the black portal, shield raised high.

"I'm with the paladin," Rings said. He was ripped and scored in a dozen places from Eidola's tentacles, but a fierce light blazed in his eyes. "Besides, why would the old builders of this place install a portal to nowhere?" He trotted forward and stepped through.

"Maybe they wanted to arrange something special for anyone who despoiled this tomb," Belgin answered, speaking to the blackness. "Maybe—oh, to hell with it." With a running start, the dandy leaped into the doorway, roaring an improvised battle cry.

Behind him, Jacob stood in the darkness of the wrecked crypt, glaring at the portal. "Damn, damn, damn," he muttered, pounding his fist against his palm. "It's not supposed to be like this." Jaw set, he picked up his great war blade and followed the others into the darkness.

Chapter 2
Down to the Crossroads

Cold beyond cold, darkness seared Belgin's flesh, and then he was through the gate. His bold battle cry faltered in the teeth of a bitter, stinging wind that scoured him with dust and sand. He raised a hand to shield his eyes and blundered forward. Crumbling old stone walls surrounded him, and overhead a brown sky billowed and seethed with the weight of wind-borne dust. No sun pierced the sandy veil, but something in the quality of the light hinted at late afternoon, maybe sunset. Where on Toril are we? he thought. Grimacing, he laughed bitterly. I've said that all my life and never really meant it before.

"Belgin! Over here!" A stout, dark shape materialized in the murk as Rings appeared. He looked past the sharper. "Where's the swordsman?"

"Right here," said Jacob, emerging from the portal behind them. A rune-carved arch marked the gate's location, twin to the one they'd left behind in the dungeons beneath Aetheric's palace. The fighter's golden mane whipped around his head in the relentless wind. "Not a volcano, not a dragon's den," he remarked. "I guess this could have been worse."

"That depends on how you look at it," Belgin said. "Eidola's out of our cage now." He turned his back on Jacob and Rings, moving forward to examine their surroundings. The ground was broken and rugged, heaps of uneven stone piled at random all around him. The walls seemed to form a large courtyard with rows of broken columns rising from drifts and skeletal fingers clawing up through the hissing, shifting sands. Beyond the old walls he gained glimpses of the dark bulk of neighboring structures, revealed and then hidden by the dust. No, not a courtyard, he decided. It's a great building, long since collapsed. I'm standing on the rubble of the roof. He scanned the wreckage again, still trying to absorb his surroundings. He'd seen blood and horror and death aplenty in the last few days, but as he gazed on the ruins, he felt as if he were a ghost moving in a sad and silent phantom world. He'd left his capacity for wonder too far behind.

Rings scrambled up to stand beside him, Jacob following a step behind. The three stood together a moment, the wind howling mournfully around them. "What is this place?" Rings asked softly.

"Who cares? It's long dead," said Jacob. "Faerûn is choked with ruins such as these."

Belgin scratched at the two-day stubble on his round jaw, narrowing his eyes against the dust and sand. "A temple, I think," he said, ignoring Jacob. "The portal we came through opened when the tomb was disturbed. Guarding the places of the dead is traditionally a role for priests or those who might serve them."

"They haven't been very attentive of late, have they?" Jacob laughed.

"Don't be so sure, Jacob. A thousand years is a long time to wait, but some guardians might have the patience for the vigil." Belgin turned in a slow circle, studying the maze of rubble around them. Perhaps it was only the melancholy sighing of the wind in the old stone that unsettled him . . . or maybe something else, something more sentient and aware. He knew enough about places such as this to feel a distinct chill at the wind's soulless moaning.

"Miltiades comes," announced Rings. The dwarf's brass and gold piercings gleamed in the fading sunlight. From the swirling murk that marked the temple's ancient gate the paladin wearily strode, a tall shape gleaming with silver.

"See Eidola?" Miltiades asked without preamble.

"No," said Jacob. "I take it you didn't, either. What happened to you?"

"She was only a few steps ahead when we emerged from the portal, but she outran me, and I lost sight of her," Miltiades admitted. "She's hiding somewhere in the ruins. Come on, let's get moving. We can't let her get too far ahead of us." He turned away and set out toward the gate, hammer resting over his shoulder.

"Miltiades, wait," Belgin called. "We have to talk." He glanced at Rings standing beside him.

The paladin paused, looking back over his shoulder. "We don't have time to talk, pirate. Keep up or turn back, but don't stay the course of Tyr's justice."

"Justice?" Belgin asked. "Look at yourself, man. You left your reason at the door when we set off on this little expedition. What were you thinking, running off alone after a creature like Eidola? What if she'd doubled back on you? She could have killed you alone in the ruins, while we stood here wondering where you'd gone."

"For that matter, how do we know that you're not Eidola in Miltiades's shape?" Rings asked suspiciously. He leaped down the stone pile, rock skittering under his feet. "Eh? Can you prove that you're not? You've been out of sight of all of us for a good ten minutes now."

"I'm not a doppelganger," Miltiades growled. "Now, come on! We don't have time for this. I need your help to find her."

"Make the time," Rings stated flatly. He slowly drew his axe from his belt. "I've had all I can stomach of shapechangers."

"How in Tyr's name can I prove that I'm not a doppelganger?" Miltiades roared. "Stand here and *not* change my shape?"

"Work a magic of Tyr," Jacob suggested. The lean fighter circled wide, moving to leave himself plenty of room to wield his man-high great sword. Belgin noticed that the fighter had his eyes on the rogues as well as the paladin. "What of you two? Can you show that you're not shapeshifters?"

"Good," Belgin said. "Don't trust any of us. I'll make a point of not trusting any of you, and we'll all get on famously." He turned back to Miltiades. "I don't think we'll need you to work a miracle, Miltiades. Just answer me this question: Where did we first meet?"

"Doegan, of course," the paladin answered.

"Better than that, Miltiades. Exactly where and when?"

With an annoyed look, Miltiades deliberately said, "We met in battle in the court of the fountain, two days ago. I fought Entreri until Noph interfered, lassoing us with his magical lariat."

"Good enough for me," Belgin replied slowly. He took his hand from the hilt of his sword. "I don't think Eidola could have known that. Now, what do you want to do, paladin?"

"Wait a minute," Rings said. "So we believe Miltiades is Miltiades. How does he know he can trust us?"

"Tyr guides me," the paladin answered bluntly. One by one, he studied Rings, Belgin, then Jacob. To his surprise, Belgin felt uneasy beneath Miltiades's unblinking gaze, as if his darkest secrets were laid bare for the paladin to see. The tall warrior allowed his eyes to rest on

Jacob a moment longer and then stated, "I see no evil in your hearts. You're all who you say you are."

"Fine, fine, so everyone's what they seem," Jacob said. "Now what?"

"We search the city for Eidola, house by house if we have to," Miltiades replied. He sighed and leaned his warhammer against one wall, sitting on a windswept stone. "But first, I think we need to rest a short time. I thank you, Belgin—I've allowed anger to rule me for too long."

"Think nothing of it." Belgin shrugged his satchel from his hip and collapsed to the ground, while his companions followed suit. He allowed himself a sparse drink of water and gnawed at a piece of dried sausage from his stores. Exhausted, he leaned his head against the cold stone. *I hope she's as tired as I am,* he thought. *Tyr knows it would only be fair.* He laughed weakly at the unspoken prayer to a god he didn't venerate, but the cloying sand caught in his throat. The vicious coughing fit left him helpless for several minutes, his chest aching abominably. Gasping for breath, Belgin tried to pretend he couldn't feel the rasp in his lungs.

"Are you ill?" Miltiades asked, studying him closely.

"He's from Edenvale," Rings answered for him.

"What's that mean?"

"It means that I'm dying," Belgin said weakly. "It's the damned bloodforges. Doegan has its fish scales . . . and lately the black malaise that incapacitated the warriors of the city. In Konigheim, it's a weakness of the will or the mind . . . everyone knows a Konigheimer who's snapped."

"Including Kurthe," Rings muttered.

Belgin nodded. "Some say Konigheimers have been known to grow a third eye. I don't know about that, though."

"Edenvale's curse is simple," Belgin continued. "We just die young. That's it. My father died at thirty-three, my mother at thirty-one. My grandsire, he lived to be forty-one. He was accounted lucky. Everyone pays the price for our kings' toys."

Miltiades and Jacob stared at him in silence for a long moment. "How old are you now?" the paladin asked.

"Thirty-four. I guess all the time I spent at sea's been good for my health. I'd probably be dead by now if I'd stayed at home."

"Tyr has the power to heal—" the paladin began.

"Not this," Belgin interrupted. "It's a curse, a magical curse. Believe me, plenty of our priests have tried to undo the bloodforge's effects. I don't know of any who have succeeded."

"Tyr grant that Kern destroys that infernal device. And any others that remain in the Utter East, for that matter. Nothing could be worth that cost." Miltiades stood, his face set in a stonelike expression. "Can you continue?"

"I'll live. For now, anyway," Belgin said with a grimace of false bravado. Although his hands trembled with the palsy of an old man, the sharper pushed himself to his feet and retrieved his satchel. "Don't worry, Miltiades—I mean to make sure the doppelganger doesn't outlive me. Lead the way."

* * * * *

Moving slowly now, the two warriors and the two pirates sallied from the old temple into the stone city. As Belgin feared, the howling wind erased tracks almost as soon as they were made; Eidola's trail was nonexistent. They circled the ancient shrine, searching the buildings nearby to no effect. Again Belgin felt a cold tone in the wind, a hint of malice and solidity that plucked at his cloak like a living thing, but it vanished before he could even say a word of warning to the others. *What kind of guardians watched the crypt we disturbed?* he thought. *Could they still be here?*

The outer buildings seemed more intact than the central temple. Smaller and sturdier, some even retained their roofs. Beyond the ring of buildings there was a large open space and a crumbling wall that seemed to circle the whole set of ruins. Broken and buried in drifting sand, nothing but desolate sand and flat sheets of rock stretched out beyond the walls. After one deliberate circuit, they paused in the lee of the outer wall, considering their next move. "This place isn't a city," Rings observed. "There aren't enough dwellings or private buildings."

"A temple complex or holy city, then," Miltiades said. "Deliberately removed from the mundane world, isolated as a retreat for worship and ceremony."

"It would be appropriate for a city of the dead," the dwarf added. "The builders interred their kings and nobles in a sacred city far from the common folk. They could hide the tombs anywhere in Faerûn with those magical gates."

"Who would go to that much trouble?" Jacob asked.

"I can think of someone," Belgin said. "The mage lords of ancient Netheril."

"Netheril?" Jacob guffawed. "Tell me another tale, charlatan."

"The statues in the tomb we found were carved in the mode of ancient Netherese dress," Belgin said, tugging at his ear. "The runes and hieroglyphs marking the portal, they were Netherese as well. And I've seen a few faint traces of more hieroglyphs in walls sheltered from the wind. Besides . . . we're sitting in the middle of a desert. If these are Netherese ruins, I'd expect we're somewhere in Anauroch."

Rings stared at Belgin. "What's a Netherese? And where in the Five Kingdoms is Anauroch?"

The sharper shrugged. "I'm no expert, Rings. I'm just guessing. But Netheril was once a great empire ruled by mighty wizards, far to the northwest of the Five Kingdoms . . . fairly close to the homeland of these gentlemen, in fact," he said, nodding at Miltiades and Jacob. "A long time ago, the Netherese brought some kind of awful magical doom down on their heads, and their kingdom fell, only to be buried by the sand and rock of the desert called Anauroch."

"I've traveled Anauroch before," Miltiades said. "I've never seen this particular place, but it feels right. How did you learn of these things, Belgin?"

"I was given an unusual education." Belgin spread his hands with a disarming gesture. "I've read a hundred books and learned a thousand tales. But just as my old mentor predicted, I've wasted my learning on a life of iniquity, deceit, and moral ambiguity." He grinned abruptly. "If only she could see me now, battling fiends and consorting with paladins. She might think I'd turned out right after all."

"Do any of your tales offer insight into the catching of doppelgangers?"

"Nothing as practical as that, I fear," Belgin said.

"Then I think it's time I called on Tyr to aid us in our quest," Miltiades said. Standing, the paladin raised his warhammer, his lips moving in silent prayer. The seething brown murk seemed to lift for just a moment, and his silver armor gleamed scarlet in the setting sun. Opening his eyes, he turned to face the old ruins, seeming to search the dusty arcades and plazas with a sense keener than mortal sight. "She's in that direction," he stated with confidence. "Tyr has granted me a seeking-spell, and I can sense the lariat that binds the doppelganger."

"How far off?" Rings asked, scrambling to his feet.

"Not far," Miltiades answered. He glanced over his shoulder at the ruddy glow along the western horizon, the only hint of the sun they'd seen in hours. "If we move fast, we can confront the doppelganger before darkness falls."

* * * * *

The four glided through the ruins, intent on their goal. They trailed quietly down a narrow alleyway drifted knee-deep in soft sand, crossed the shell of an old barracks house, then padded across an open boulevard lined with shattered columns. The stump of a round tower rose ahead of them, above the low rooftops and dunes. Miltiades raised his hand and crouched low behind a ruined colonnade. The others followed his lead.

He nodded at the tower and whispered, "In there.

Remember, she's caught by Noph's magical rope. If you can lay hold of it, she'll be powerless to resist, and we can take her back to Waterdeep."

Rings glanced at Belgin. The sharper returned his gaze without expression, and the dwarf silently nodded in agreement, drawing his axe from his belt loop. She won't be standing trial if Rings or I have anything to say about it, he decided. They weren't being paid to pass judgment, only to execute the judgment their unknown employer had decided upon.

"We're ready," Belgin said.

Miltiades stood and vaulted over the stone block, dashing for the splintered doorway as if his armor of silver plate was a light cloak. Belgin and Rings ran after the paladin, while Jacob brought up the rear at a more cautious pace, keeping an eye on the dismal ruins and howling sand behind them. The great paladin stormed the dark tower like a righteous hurricane, the pirates only a step behind him.

They caught Eidola in her natural shape. Gray and gaunt, she was a skeletal creature draped in loose, leathery flesh. The lariat still circled her neck, although she'd carefully coiled the trailing end and secured it by her side. Hissing in rage, she crouched like a monstrous spider and whirled to face Miltiades as the paladin charged straight at her.

"Insolent human! What must I do to teach you to stay out of my path?" she howled.

"Surrender, monster! We have you trapped!" Miltiades shouted. He leaped forward, attacking in a deadly hail of hammer blows. Lithe and quick, the gray creature eluded the first rush, and then there were two Miltiades, identical to each other, flailing away with silver hammers.

Belgin checked his own rush, Rings hesitating as well. "Which one is real?" the dwarf roared in frustration.

"I am!" cried one Miltiades.

"Don't listen to him!" answered the other.

The sharper looked at the dwarf and said, "Don't tell me you didn't expect that."

Scowling, he circled the battling paladins, rapier at

the ready. Rings grunted and followed his lead. Behind them, Jacob filled the doorway, watching the fight as he tried to gauge which one to strike at. Belgin glanced around the room, measuring the arena. The tower's floor was choked with rough rubble; its stone walls rose only twenty or thirty feet before ending in a jagged stump. The walls above them glowed orange with the last rays of the sunset. One Miltiades stumbled but parried the other's attack and drove his reflection back toward Rings. "Think, lad, think!" Belgin muttered to himself. "Which one's real?"

The dwarf raised his axe but held his blow, cursing. "I don't know which one to hit!"

"I know a way to find out," Belgin said, smiling grimly. "Miltiades, don't say anything. Eidola? Which one are you?"

"I am," said the Miltiades with his back to Rings.

Instantly the dwarf swung his axe in a low, vicious cut, but Miltiades-Eidola leaped over the blow and quickly grappled with the real Miltiades, spinning around. Belgin slashed at the imposter as the two reeled close to him and was rewarded with a hiss of pain. Dark blood stained his sword blade, and the battling paladins moved away again, locked in their deadly embrace.

From the doorway, Jacob surged forward. "I've got her!" he cried. He raised his mighty war blade for a monstrous stroke certain to cut the doppelganger in two.

"No, Jacob! That's the wrong one!" Belgin shouted in alarm.

Undeterred, the Tyrian warrior lashed out, the blade flashing like a gleam of doom in the dusk. At the last instant, the Miltiades he struck dropped to one knee and used his hammer to turn the blade aside, though not before the tip of Jacob's sword cut a long, shallow gash down his face. Bright red human blood splashed the sand.

"Jacob!" Miltiades cried. "You almost killed me!"

Miltiades-Eidola stepped forward to strike at her foe's back, but Belgin and Rings moved in from the flank, driving her back. Suddenly they faced the gray doppelganger again as she abandoned her imitation of the paladin. She bared her fangs in a fierce snarl, then whirled and leaped high into the air, catching hold of the worn stone of the tower's wall. Like a great insect she scuttled upward, fashioning hooks and loops from her hands to speed her climb. In the blink of an eye she'd vanished over the wall's broken parapet, thirty feet above.

"She's fled outside!" Belgin called. "Come on! She's wounded!"

Shaken, the real Miltiades rose, one hand pressed to his bleeding face. He glared at Jacob, then pushed past the fighter without saying a word. He paused in the tower's door and scanned the darkening city. "She's moving," he stated flatly, then vanished into the street beyond.

Belgin quickly followed, keeping Miltiades in sight. Behind him, Rings caught Jacob's arm and spun the fighter to face him. Despite the difference in their stature, the dwarf forced the fighter to meet his eyes. "You idiot," he snapped. "We had her! Have you got rocks between your ears?"

Jacob's face whitened, and the warrior tore out of Rings's grasp. He angrily slammed his mailed fist against the ancient wall, flailing at his own mistake. "I know what I did," he retorted. Then he bolted out the door after the other two. Rings lowered his head and charged in pursuit, refusing to be left behind.

They ran through the dusty streets, following the silver gleam of Miltiades. The paladin halted in a stone plaza before an old palace, closing his eyes to sense the magical lariat. Belgin skidded to a stop beside him, scanning the plaza with his eyes. There! A dark shape slipped up the weathered stairs of the palace.

"Forget your divination," the sharper said, catching Miltiades's arm and pointing. "She's gone in there!"

"After her!" Miltiades sprinted across the plaza and up the steps. Belgin loped after him. Jacob and Rings, a short distance behind, altered their course and ran toward the palace.

On the horizon, the red crescent of the sun slid beneath the earth. In that moment, everything changed. The wind, quiet and sad, instantly returned with a screaming, stinging gale of hard-driven sand, catching their cloaks with ghostly talons. Driven dust and sand obscured the square in the space of moments, blinding and disorienting paladin and pirate both. The temperature of the air dropped abruptly, as if they'd waded into a stream of icy water. And the watchful, mournful presence Belgin had sensed earlier suddenly seemed tangible and malevolent, a cold and hateful thing that closed on them with the fall of darkness.

"Miltiades!" he shrieked, though his words were torn away by the wind.

The paladin stumbled on the steps. Belgin scuttled toward him, keeping low to the ground. He turned once to shout encouragement to Jacob and Rings, but the return of the storm plunged the Netherese temple into impenetrable gloom. The fighter and the dwarf were nowhere in sight—but the more he looked, the more certain he became that something was moving towards him in the roiling murk. Coughing, he drew a silken scarf from his collar and pulled it up over his nose and mouth.

"Do you feel it, paladin?" he called to Miltiades, a few feet away.

"I feel it, Belgin," Miltiades answered. His voice was distant and faint, even though he shouted to raise his voice above the storm. "The evil of this place sleeps no longer!"

"What is it?"

"I know not!" The paladin scrambled to his feet, spinning to search the ruins with an arm raised to shield his eyes. "Where are Jacob and Rings?"

"They were thirty or forty yards behind me, in the middle of the square. They can't be far!"

"They must have gotten turned around in the dust," Miltiades said. He stood, buffeted by the vicious wind. Sand hissed from his armor like the sound of rain falling on a hot skillet. For the first time, Belgin saw human hesitation, human frailty, in the paladin's face. He glanced toward the empty storm behind them, up to the dark doorway at the top of the steps, then toward the square again. "Jacob!" he cried. "Rings! Are you out there?"

"They'll never hear you in this," Belgin said. "Do we look for them, or do we stay put?"

"We're all blind in this Tyr-cursed dust storm. We could spend the whole night blundering around looking for each other."

"Split up, then? You pursue the doppelganger, while I wait here for the others?"

"No, that's too dangerous. You said yourself that we can't be caught alone by her, and there's something else here, Belgin, something that awoke when the sun vanished below the sands. I can feel it seeking us. If I left you here alone, I don't think I'd ever see you again."

"Then let's leave Eidola to whatever it is that watches this place, find our comrades, and get out of here," Belgin said, raising his voice to carry over the wind. "We can return at sunrise to see if the doppelganger's still alive."

"No," said Miltiades. "No monster, no fiend, no force in this world will sway me from my course." He turned back to the crumbling palace and battled up the steps, "Come on; Eidola is somewhere within. Jacob and Rings know our quest. They must fend for themselves."

Chapter 3
Dark Designs

Night and chaos descended like the fall of a titan's maul. Trotting across the ancient square a few feet behind Jacob, Rings could see Miltiades and Belgin racing up the broken steps of an old palace, darting toward a gaping, shadowed archway. Then the sight was erased by a gust of wind powerful enough to spin him half around and blind him with an eyeful of grit. His world narrowed to a dimensionless sphere of dust, sand, and the old flagstones under his feet. "What now?" he growled aloud, even though the wind stole his words away.

He caught a glimpse of a dim, metallic gleam off to

his left and moved toward it. He bared his teeth in anger and drove his stocky frame through the storm, until a tall, ragged shape appeared suddenly from the mist. Jacob whirled to face him, greatsword at the ready. "Who goes there?" the human challenged.

"Who do you think?" Rings answered. "Hold your blade, numbskull."

Jacob scowled fiercely but lowered his sword. "Where did this come from?" he shouted, waving one hand to indicate the brown gloom that surrounded them.

"I think that Belgin's guardians have finally taken note of us," Rings answered. "Maybe they were waiting for the sun to go down. Can you see or hear the others?"

"I can't see my hand in front of my face. The last I saw, Miltiades and the dandy ran into a building over that way."

Rings eyed Jacob's choice of direction. "Are you sure? I thought it was over there."

The fighter nodded. "I'm sure of it. I was looking right at them when darkness fell."

"Okay, I'll take your word for it. Let's get out of this damned dust."

Jacob glanced around once more to fix his bearings, then moved off into the murk, leaning into the wind. Rings followed, one hand resting on the fighter's pack. They seemed to walk for a long time before they encountered a low, stone parapet that ran until it vanished in the gloom to either side.

"This can't be right," Rings said. "The building we seek had a long colonnade and a big staircase in front of it."

"I think I saw this wall on the left side of the square. We need to follow it toward the right to get to the palace."

"I don't remember any damned wall at all," Rings snorted. "I think this is going to be a lot harder than we thought."

"Well, do you want to lead?" Jacob snapped.

"At least I know when I'm lost. Try it your way; maybe you're right after all."

Jacob looked left, then started along the wall toward the right, trailing his left hand along the old stone. Again, they seemed to walk a long time. The world ceased beyond the five or ten feet they could see around them, but Rings began to suspect that something or someone trailed them just out of sight, moving in and out of the corners of his perception like a half-remembered nightmare.

"My eyes are beginning to play tricks on me," the dwarf said, as quietly as he could over the roaring of the wind.

"Mine, too," Jacob said. He halted and moved a step from the wall, giving himself space to wield his two-handed sword. "Show yourselves!" he shouted in challenge. "Come on!"

Rings automatically turned and put his back to the tall warrior, guarding his flank. At the fringe of his vision he saw them now, brown and withered figures that approached in fluttering tatters of cloth and flesh. They were long dead, of course, silent phantoms with cruel talons and eyes that burned like witch fire. Rings balanced his fighting axe in his right hand and crouched, ready to strike. "How many on your side?" he asked.

"Enough," Jacob answered. "And you?"

"More than enough," Rings answered. The first mummy reached him, clubbing its knotted fists down at his head. He twisted aside and took the corpse's leg off at the knee with one swift stroke, then ducked under the swing of a rust-flaked sword that broke on the wall beside him. He hewed the ancient warrior's arm from its body, then stumbled to the ground as the first one he'd felled tripped him with its grappling talons. Cold, bony claws raked deep into the flesh of his thigh, and Rings gagged in pain and revulsion. He smashed the creature's skull with one blow of his axe and pried its talons from his leg while the next one advanced to attack. "Jacob!" he called.

There was no reply. Rings staggered back a step, drove off the next dead one with a flurry of slashes, then risked a glance over his shoulder. Half a dozen of the ancient dead lay in the sand, hacked limb from limb, and in the swirling darkness he thought he saw a gleam of white movement as the Tyrian warrior danced and spun among the relentless horde, blade flashing. "Jacob! Stay close!" Rings shouted. Then he had to turn back to defend himself from an ancient priest-thing that attacked him with a heavy bronze sceptre. When next he looked, he could see nothing of Jacob at all.

More of the dead warriors closed in on him, forcing him to turn constantly, defending his flank and back. Rings howled a challenge that was swept away by the voiceless wind, smashed a hulking warrior to the ground, then turned again to put the stone of the old wall to his shoulders. His outstretched fingers felt nothing but emptiness behind him; there was a breach in the wall, and no foes in the gloom beyond.

Rings didn't waste a moment; he turned and ran for his life, hoping that there was nothing worse in the gloom than the horror of walking dead he'd left behind him. He floundered past blank stone and hissing sand, scratched and clawed in a dozen places. "Belgin! Miltiades! Jacob!" he called, staggering through the ruins. "Belgin!"

There was no reply.

* * * * *

The paladin and the sharper advanced cautiously into the Netherese palace, tendrils of sand shifting and dancing around their feet as the wind howled through the doorway and clutched at their cloaks. The room beyond was a shallow portico, with tall columns carved into the image of ancient warriors supporting a low ceiling of heavy stone block. Three passageways led into the building, dark and dusty in the deepening gloom.

"Which way?" asked Belgin.

Miltiades turned his head from side to side, concentrating. "Straight ahead," he replied. They moved down a long hall decorated with ancient frescoes that still held a hint of their color, showing cryptic scenes of bronze-skinned people in cotton kilts. Some fought in great battles; others worked in broad fields of grain; a few stood above the others conjuring mighty spells out of the air. The passage came to an abrupt end at an archway framed by rough-dressed stone. A narrow flight of steps ran down into the darkness beyond. "She's down there somewhere."

"Great," muttered Belgin. "Another dungeon, or crypt, or subterranean hall of horrors. Why don't creatures of irredeemable evil ever set up house in some pleasant, sunny spot?"

"You wouldn't take them seriously if they did," Miltiades replied.

Hammer at the ready, he advanced down the stair, crouching to avoid striking his head on the low ceiling. Belgin followed, trailing his free hand along the wall. After twenty or thirty steps, the passage opened in a broad hall lined with rows of plain stone columns. Around the perimeter of the room dozens of blank stone archways were evely spaced along the wall, each surrounded by an intricate ring of rune-etched stone. The long, low chamber extended into the darkness.

"These look familiar," breathed Belgin quietly.

"Aye. More portals," Miltiades agreed. "Where do they all go?"

The sharper moved closer to the nearest portal and carefully brushed the dust from its circle of runes. He traced the inscription with one finger, whispering under his breath, then stepped back. "This one goes to Chessenta, I think. Or an old Mulhorese ruin that I've heard of that lies in that land." He moved over to the next one, scrutinizing it carefully. "Here's one that goes to a place called Myth Drannor. Ever hear of it?"

"Don't open it!" Miltiades barked quickly. "It wouldn't make things any better."

"I'm not sure I could even if I wanted to. Gates such as these often need very specific keys to open. Unless the builders of these archways were kind enough to hide the activating phrase in these inscriptions . . ." The sharper turned back to study the archway.

Miltiades watched Belgin for a long moment. The ancient hieroglyphs meant nothing to him, preceding the ancient days in which he'd led his first life by thousands of years. His eyes narrowed in suspicion as Belgin moved to the next archway and softly traced the stone carving. "Hold, scoundrel!" he cried, darting forward to catch the sharper by the wrist. "You worked magic to comprehend these runes!"

"Tyr has no problem with the practice of magic, does he?" Belgin answered angrily, pulling his hand from Miltiades's grasp. "How could I read this gibberish otherwise?"

"Tyr takes no offense at the working of magic, but he does have a problem with deception," grated the paladin. "Who are you, pirate? What are you doing here? Explain yourself!"

Belgin straightened and drew back his shoulders, a scowl settling over his round face. "What do you care?" he said sharply. "I'm exactly what you see—a pirate, a cutthroat, a dandy and a sharp. I take from those too weak or too stupid to defend themselves. I've stolen from kings and from beggars. I've killed good men and bad. I've reneged on my bargains, lied to those who trusted me, turned my back on those in need. Sometimes I've dared a deed worthy of a song, and more often I've murdered a song before it was born. That's who I am, paladin. If you don't like it, keep your judgments to yourself."

"You have led an unjust life," said Miltiades.

"Well, life's been unjust to me."

"You feel remorse," the paladin said.

"What does it matter if I do? It's a vanity of mine."

"No, it's not vanity. I know evil when I see it, Belgin. That's the weight and the gift of paladinhood. And whatever you think, evil isn't in your heart."

You've got to be kidding me. Belgin almost laughed, but his damaged lungs could only manage a shallow wheeze. "It's a bit late to save me, paladin, although I'm sure my mother'd thank you for trying."

Miltiades laughed quietly. "Fine. So how much do you

know of magic?"

"Only a smattering. I've knowledge of about a dozen spells, none suitable for battling a creature such as Eidola. Most of my magic is in illusion and charms."

"How did a pirate come to learn the wizard's art?"

Belgin straightened, a grimace of pain flitting across his face. "You'd be surprised at how far a little illusion magic goes at the card table, or at what a swindler can do with a simple charm." *How's that for irony?* he thought. *I can't even take a shill without cheating somehow.* He laughed again, his strength returning. "Besides, I wasn't always a pirate. I learned what I know years before I came aboard the *Kissing Shark*." Suddenly the pirate straightened, looking back toward the passage they'd descended. Something dragged softly on the stone steps above.

The paladin opened his mouth, but Belgin silenced him with an upraised hand. The air grew cold, and the bitter chill threatened to start him coughing again. "We're not alone," he whispered.

"I feel it, Belgin." Biting his lip, the paladin stepped away from the door. He glanced around, then nodded across the dark hall. "I still sense Eidola in that direction. Come on." Leaving the stair behind, they crossed the hall of pillars, only to find another stair leading up.

Bounding up the steps, they emerged into the shrieking chaos of the sandstorm. They stood in the ruins of a small shrine or stone patio, its roof long since gone. Belgin could feel something climbing steadily up the dark steps behind them, deliberate and unhurried. "Where's the doppelganger?" he shouted at Miltiades.

"I'm not sure. She's moving again!"

"Well, pick a direction! I don't want to find out what's behind us!"

Miltiades glanced over his shoulder at the dark stairway, then scanned the rubble around them. His eye fell on a drum-shaped piece of masonry, evidently once a piece of a pillar. He stumbled over to the stone and tried to lift it. "Help me!" he cried. Belgin scrambled over and joined him. Together they flipped the stone onto its edge and hauled it to the top of the steps.

Green-glowing eyes looked up at them as something clad in ancient bronze climbed toward them, a long glaive of emerald fire burning in its yellowed hands. More eyes glinted in the darkness beneath it. The paladin and the sharper exchanged one look, then set their shoulders to the stone. It teetered for a moment on the topmost step and then tipped over, rolling down the stairs with an ear-shattering clatter. The skeletal warriors moved slowly to avoid the block, but there was no room to dodge. In a roar of dust and stone they were swept away down the stairs.

"What was that?" Belgin panted as the resounding echoes died away.

"You don't want to know," Miltiades answered. He straightened, setting a hand to his back with a wince. "I'm getting too old for this. Come on. Eidola's somewhere in that direction."

Staggering against the storm's rage, they blundered out into the ancient streets.

* * * * *

Jacob slashed his way clear of the dessicated mummies with a burst of superhuman speed and strength, leaving a dozen or more of the ancient warriors dismembered in the sand-swept street. For the moment, no enemies stalked him. Shielding his frail human eyes with an upraised arm, he trudged back into the wind, seeking the colonnaded palace. Rings he dismissed as dead; if the creatures that had attacked them didn't get the dwarf, something else surely would. Jacob could sense the malignant sentience behind the sandstorm and the walking dead, and it seemed likely it would try to isolate and destroy them. "Well, feel free to try," he snorted into the storm. "I've a surprise or two for you, whatever you are."

The storm didn't bother to reply. Jacob shrugged and continued, feeling his way across the open square. A dark shape loomed up out of the gloom, with another behind it, and a third dimly visible behind that—a row of columns, standing on a stone porch. "I'll be damned,"

Jacob muttered. Now, which way? He'd been wrong before and gone too far to the right, which meant that he needed to follow the portico to the left to find the doorway inside . . . or so he thought. He decided to turn left and slogged on through the drifting sand, keeping the columns in sight.

A prickling in the back of his neck warned him of danger. Whirling, he lashed out with his sword, just in time to meet the attack of a tall, powerful mummy with eyes of green flame. The undead thing hissed in frustration as white steel met the fall of its black scythe and pressed closer, drawing back for another strike. Jacob scrambled back for space to fight, slipped on the stone steps, and fell back into the sand. Dazed, he shook his head to clear his vision.

The ancient warrior towered over him, scythe poised for the kill. "I don't think so," Jacob said. With boneless ease he shifted his form, instantly transforming his left arm into a steel spear and punching it through the mummy's empty skull. The withered torso collapsed like a puppet with its strings cut. Jacob quickly resumed his original form and stood, looking around for the next attack.

"Very good," said a voice behind him, cutting through the wind like a blade of cold steel. Jacob turned slowly, a feral grin on his features. Watching from the shadows of the colonnade stood an athletic human woman in black leather, a strand of hemp hiding at her collar. "I didn't expect that."

"I've been looking for you," Jacob said.

Interlude
... Of Monsters and Men

Portals, portals everywhere. Which one do I seek?

Eidola won't do for this. She's strong, swift, and beautiful, but she doesn't know a thing about the works of ancient Netheril or the crafting of spells. The minotaur and the mastiff are useless now, the cuttlefish demon too. The great fiend? No, it was merely a shell. If I'd really conquered a balor, I'd have no need of a wizard's magic—I could walk the planes by wishing it so. It was good enough to get me past the fiends that swarmed through Aetheric's dungeons, but I'm not a balor. Not even close.

But Jarin, on the other hand . . . Jarin has served me well on many occasions. His knowledge of sorcery is impressive for one so young. He'll have the knowledge I seek.

Before I crafted Eidola, Jarin was a persona I used quite often. It takes only a moment of concentration to shape the familiar features, the hawklike gaze, the handsome face. My mind takes the shape of his, and knowledge floods into my brain. I've forgotten how to disarm a swordsman with a twist of my wrist, I've forgotten how to mend damaged mail and how to kill with blows of my bare human fists—but I remember now the Art, and a dozen languages long forgotten, and the sensation of Mystra's weave gliding beneath the touch of my fingers and the force of my will. It might be the next best thing to my true self.

As Jarin, the faded hieroglyphs suddenly take on meaning. Myth Drannor. Cormanthyr. Menzoberrazan. Oh, if only I'd known of this place years ago! The Netherese must have scattered tombs across all of Faerûn and perhaps even farther, to judge by these names I don't know. What cult or sect went to this trouble? Who did they inter in this fashion, and why? And how—

Enough. That's the curiosity of Jarin. I need an answer, not a history lesson. The paladin and his ally will track me soon enough. I could probably defeat them now, but Miltiades has a nasty habit of surviving. Better to leave him here if I can, or to face him on familiar territory if he still follows.

Here. The Hall of Swords. A portal leading to the heart of Undermountain! Who could have guessed that even in the depths of the Mad Mage's domain a Netherese lord sleeps? It's amazing that Faerûn holds together, considering how it's been riddled with gates and conduits, portals and doorways from a dozen lost peoples. If I had anything like a sense of wonder, I might be impressed.

Instead, I search for the portal's key. Jarin has spells to reveal such things. Best to move swiftly, before the paladin returns.

Raising Jarin's hands, I begin to weave a spell.

Chapter 4
Masks and Machinations

"Eidola's gone!" Miltiades halted in the lee of an old wall, dropping to one knee. Before him, lying half-buried in the sand, he saw the pale outline of Noph's lasso. In frustration the tall paladin slammed one armored fist against the wall and turned his face away from the stinging sand. "How could she have freed herself from the rope?"

Belgin crouched next to him, taking what shelter he could from the weathered stones. The sharper rubbed at his jaw, frowning at the gritty coating of sand that came away with his hand. He ran his fingers through his hair and realized that he'd been thoroughly covered in dust and grit. How about a long holiday when this is all over, my boy? he thought ruefully. "Did you know Eidola to work magic?"

"No, as Eidola she has no such skill," Miltiades replied. "I saw her fight against Aetheric's minions when she was abducted. The sword, not the spell, was her weapon."

"Then the only thing I can think of is that she somehow found someone or something to command the lasso to release her. Damn the luck!" He paused, then added, "Can you shift the target of your seeking spell?"

"No, I can only perceive the first object that I decide to seek."

"She could be anywhere," Belgin muttered. He reached down and picked up the lasso, coiling it at his belt. "I guess I'll give this back to Noph if—damn!"

"What? What is it?" Miltiades asked.

"We've got another problem, Miltiades," the sharper said. "Why would Eidola abandon the lasso once she'd escaped from it? Magic of this sort is too valuable and rare to leave lying about, after all."

"She left it here because we were using it to track her movements."

"And how could she have known that?" Belgin asked bitterly.

The paladin stared at the sharper blankly for a long moment, and then sighed. "Jacob or Rings. She must have defeated one or both of them." He worked his fists together, slamming metal into metal as he thought furiously.

"Which way now?" Belgin asked quietly.

"Back to the palace," Miltiades said. "If I were her, I'd double back and try to find a portal that led to someplace else. Besides, that's where Rings and Jacob are most likely to look for us, if they still live."

"It's as good a guess as any."

They pushed off into the storm again, trying to feel their way back toward the palace. Belgin found himself throwing frequent glances over his shoulder. He hadn't forgotten the undead things that followed them up out of the hall of doors, and the storm around them seemed to hiss and coil with a sentient malevolence. *If I had a lick of sense, I'd leave Miltiades to his vendetta and leave this hateful old ruin miles behind me,* he thought.

As if he'd stumbled into an unseen razor of steel, bitter cold and visceral horror slid through the sharper's heart. The raging storm seemed to recoil as they stumbled into a clearing of unnatural calm, but the wild and random malevolence that shrieked and wailed all around them seemed to coalesce into a single presence, looming in the ash and dust ahead. Belgin opened his mouth to make light of the creeping horror around them, but for once he had nothing to say.

The whirling dust clouds parted, revealing a tattered brown figure dressed in the cerements of the tomb. Eyes of living green flame blazed in its sunken orbits, frozen emeralds dancing in an open grave. Regal trappings of gold, tarnished and ancient, marked the creature as a great lord of vanished Netheril. A grim company of lesser undead flanked the master, their eyes flickering with dim echoes of the malevolence that burned in their lord's face.

Thy hour is done, mortals. The creature's whisper rasped inside Belgin's mind like the husk of a dead insect. *No man may walk the streets of Ularith and live to tell the tale.*

"Stand aside, ancient one," said Miltiades firmly. "Our mission here does not aggrieve the dead of Ularith. We seek a fugitive who has fled to this place, and we shall leave the instant we have captured or slain her. Do not hinder us in our mission."

You dare to make demands of me? The skeletal face was incapable of expression, but the eyes burned colder and brighter than before. A nimbus of black power sprang into being around its yellowed talons, old and strong magic wielded with undying precision. *You dare?*

"Miltiades, perhaps we could state our case a little more diplomatically—" Belgin began quietly, finally finding his tongue.

The paladin ignored him. "Ancient one, I serve Tyr.

Justice is the only power I bow to, and I must do as Tyr commands me. I do not willingly intrude upon your sleep."

What do I care what upstart godling you serve, or what purpose brought you here? Your petty mortal affairs are of no concern to me. You claim to serve a power of justice, human; now hear the judgment I render against you. You and all who follow you will remain here in unending death, guarding that which you have defiled with your intrusion! From the cold depths of the city around them, rank on rank of the dead warriors appeared, advancing in lifeless unison. The lich-lord raised its hand, black death streaming from its talons.

Miltiades sighed and lowered his warhammer. Slowly, he removed his silver helm, baring his dark mane to the howling dust. He stepped forward to meet the advancing dead, virtually defenseless. "Claim me for your minion if you can, then," he said.

"Have you lost your mind?" hissed Belgin. Bronze glaives and grinning death pressed in close on all sides.

Very well, the lich agreed. It spoke a word of ancient power, and the black nimbus at its hands lanced forward in an ebon spear, striking Miltiades in the center of his chest. Cold black flames danced over the paladin. Before Belgin's eyes, the smooth muscles and firm features of the Phlanian withered into dry, sere bone as the paladin's shining armor darkened with the tarnish of ages. Miltiades stood before the Netherese lich, a skeletal remnant of the warrior that he was.

"Miltiades," whispered the sharper in horror.

I command you, the lich hissed. *Claim now your companion for me.*

"No," stated the paladin. His withered limbs seemed to lengthen and grow, clothing him in flesh once more as the patina faded from his armor. In the space of a moment he stood as a man again, his armor gleaming bright in the darkness and murk of the ruins. "I slept for six hundred years in the darkness of death, called forth from my tomb to serve Tyr when I was needed. I know what it is to be one of the ancient dead, the long and hollow wait in the darkness, the aching for the flesh long rotted away. You have no power over me, lich. Now, I ask you, let me and my companion pass."

The undead lord stood in silence a long time, its minions motionless by its side. Slowly it lowered its hands, and the cold fire in its eyes seemed to dim. *I see that you speak the truth, warrior of Tyr. You have until sunrise to finish your business in Ularith. Any who remain here when the sun rises in the morning will never leave this place, regardless of Tyr's will in the matter.*

"We will not disturb your sleep again," Miltiades said quietly.

The lich and its minions made no reply, instead fading back into the endless sandstorm. As they vanished, the storm seemed to abate in violence, the wind dying down to a steady moan as the cold and fierce watchfulness silently relented.

Belgin blew out a big breath and slumped against the wall. "I don't want to be here anymore, Miltiades," he said earnestly.

"Nor do I, Belgin."

"What was that all about? Six hundred years of death, coming out of your tomb to serve Tyr? You're as hale and hearty as anyone I've ever met."

"It wasn't always so." Miltiades replaced his helmet and retrieved his hammer. He took a few steps down the street, and then paused as he realized that Belgin wasn't following. The sharper stood by the old wall, arms folded across his chest as he awaited a longer explanation. The paladin sighed and continued, "This is my second life, Belgin. I first lived in the service of Tyr more than six hundred years ago, in the days when Phlan was young. I met my death then, in battle against the enemies of my god. But Tyr saw fit to call me back to his service as an undead warrior. Three times I rose from my crypt to quest for Tyr, only to return to my sleep when my mission was accomplished. But at the end of my last quest, Tyr rewarded my service by restoring me to life again. I have lived now five years since that day."

Belgin shuddered despite himself. "You're six hundred years old?"

"Six hundred and fifty-five, I suppose. But hundreds of those years passed unknown to me as I slept in death, awaiting Tyr's next call."

"A few days ago, Noph asked me what I'd lost in becoming a pirate. I told him I'd lost my sense of wonder, my ability to be surprised." Belgin shook his head. "Well, what do you know? I'm astonished. How could you do it, Miltiades? What did Tyr ever give you to justify six centuries in the tomb, hoping that you might serve him again?"

The paladin offered a deprecatory smile. "Whether you know it or not, Belgin, everyone serves something greater than himself. With some souls it's money, or power, or even doubt, but for those who can find faith, death holds no terror." He looked up at the sky, then studied the ruins nearby. "I've lost track of the hour," he said, changing the subject. "The lich who watches this place struck me as the type of creature who does exactly what he says he will. Let's not tempt fate."

"Agreed. It looks like the storm's clearing some. There's the palace of portals again." Together, Belgin and Miltiades trotted over to the building. It was still dark and windy in the ancient city, but at least they could now see twenty or thirty yards through the dust and sand. At the palace doorway, Belgin paused to chalk a simple rune on one pillar. "In case Rings or Jacob come this way," he explained.

"Good idea." Miltiades led the way as they retraced their steps back down the narrow stairs they'd climbed in pursuit of Eidola. Whispering a prayer to Tyr, the paladin created a soft, silver glow from the head of his warhammer, illuminating the black passageway. "Keep your eyes open, Belgin. The dead who pursued us might still wait below."

In the soft shadows, the steps under his feet caught Belgin's eye. "Wait a moment, Miltiades," he said. Turning, he stooped to examine the stairs they'd descended. "Look here. There's a layer of old dust, marked by three trails leading up—our own, the trail of a woman in riding boots, and a ragged set of prints of feet in cloth wrappings. The column we rolled down the stair covered this with a new layer of dust and debris. Here are the tracks we just made now as we came down the stairs . . . and here are the woman's prints again, over the debris but under our latest track."

"So Eidola did come this way, after we'd rolled the stone down these steps."

"Exactly. She doubled back, as you guessed she would."

Miltiades straightened. "I didn't realize you were such a tracker."

"Another of my old talents, I guess." Belgin slipped past the paladin and descended the stair, now watching for the doppelganger's trail. At the bottom of the flight they clambered over the heavy round stone and the ancient skeletons that lay crushed beneath its weight. Belgin circled the scene twice before picking up the faint impressions of Eidola's footsteps in the sand-blown floor. He followed the track into the hall of pillars as Miltiades watched warily for any new threats. "Hmmph. This is odd."

"What's that?" asked the paladin.

"The woman's footprints vanish here, replaced by a new set. A tall but lightly built elf, I'd say, probably male; the feet are too wide for an elf maid, I think."

"Eidola must have changed again. But why an elf?"

Belgin shook his head. "I've no idea. Here, she—er, he—went this way." The track meandered past dozens of portals, finally pausing in front of one, where it ended altogether. The sharper looked up at Miltiades. "He stopped here and then stepped through this portal."

"It's nothing but blank stone now."

"Well, I'll see about that," Belgin said. He studied the cryptic runes and hieroglyphs surrounding the stone archway, delicately tracing them with one finger. "Does the name Halaster the Mad mean anything to you?"

Miltiades gaped in amazement. "Halaster the Mad? This can't be!"

"It actually translates as 'The Domain of Haalvar the Mad,' but yes, that's what it says. Why? Do you know of him?"

"He is the wizard who created the dismal maze known as Undermountain, below the city of Waterdeep. Tyr curse that wretched Eidola! She's found a way home in the middle of all this ruin." Miltiades set his jaw in determination. "Can you open this door, Belgin? If Eidola returns to Waterdeep, we are lost. We'd never find her in a city that large."

"What of Rings and Jacob?"

"We can't wait. Eidola is only a few minutes ahead of us. If we hurry, we can catch her before she finds her allies in the Undermountain or escapes to blend in with the city throngs. Unless we stop her now, she can tell any tale she likes of her abduction when she returns. Who could suspect her?" The paladin doffed his helm and ran a hand through his hair. "I don't want to leave Jacob and Rings here, but I don't see an alternative. If we don't see any chance to follow Eidola on the other side, we'll come back here and try to find our companions before sunrise."

"All right," Belgin said after a long pause. "Stand back. I'll need to work a spell." With a sidelong glance at the paladin, he slowly and deliberately wove his hands together and hummed the words of one of his few useful enchantments. *Never thought I'd have a use for this again,* he thought bitterly. *The Art's soiled by my hand.* Beneath his eyes, the ancient marks seemed to glow and brighten, revealing a delicate tracery of azure that limned the doorway. The blank gray stone seemed to vanish as a sheet of impenetrable blackness ghosted into view, yawning like a tomb. *But I still remember after all these years,* Belgin thought, *no matter how I try to forget. What does that make me?*

Miltiades nodded his thanks and readied himself to enter the gate. Belgin halted him with one hand on his shoulder. "Just a moment." Kneeling on the floor, the sharper cleared a large space on the floor and retrieved a piece of chalk from his belt pouch. He scribed a large mark, with an arrow pointing at the portal and a cryptic word beneath it. "Rings and Jacob will know which way we went, if they find this place," he said. "Now we can go."

Ready for battle, the paladin and the sharper stepped through the blackness.

* * * * *

"At least the thrice-damned storm's letting up," muttered Rings, blundering through knee-deep sand and shattered walls of old brown stone. He'd fought his way clear of two more encounters with the ancient dead who watched the city, becoming completely disoriented in the process, but as the storm abated, the withered brown mummies had taken their rest. The dwarf didn't consider himself superstitious or particularly sensitive to the supernatural, but he could feel the retreat of the evil presence that haunted the ruins. Whatever it was, it was content to watch for a time.

He came to a narrow intersection and considered the streets in front of him, trying to choose. "Which way now?"

"Rings!" The dwarf whirled at the shout. Staggering through the sand-choked alleyway to his left, Jacob appeared, sword in hand. The curly-haired warrior bled freely from a nasty cut high on his head and favored his left leg with an awkward limp, but his clear blue eyes showed no sign of defeat. "I thought you dead!"

"Me, too," the dwarf answered. He raised his axe defensively, eying the human suspiciously. "You're not Eidola in disguise, are you?"

Jacob looked up sharply, then winced. "Damn. Forgot about that. You might be Eidola, too."

"Well, I know I'm not," Rings growled, "But I guess you'd have no way to know if I'm telling the truth. Now, how would Belgin sort this out?" He thought a moment, and then said, "Open your gorget and show me that you don't have a rope around your neck, and I'll do the same."

Jacob rolled his eyes, but he complied. Rings grunted, then undid his own collar to show that his own neck was bare. "Satisfied?" the Tyrian warrior asked.

"That'll do. Any idea where Belgin and Miltiades are?"

"No, but I was thinking that I'd start with the last building they went into."

Rings nodded. "They're probably long gone, but it's worth a look. Which way is it?"

"I thought dwarves didn't get lost," Jacob laughed coldly.

"Underground we don't," Rings snapped. "At night, in a sandstorm, in a set of ruins I've never seen before today, yes—I can get lost."

"The palace is straight ahead," Jacob said. Hefting his heavy war blade again, he set off down the street, moving fast. Rings had to trot to keep up with his long-legged stride. He glowered at the human's back, but Jacob paid him no more attention.

The Tyrian's intuition was correct; they traveled about fifty yards down the alley and found themselves at a narrow courtyard or portico. The back side of the column-bordered palace loomed over an open space littered with broken masonry. Rings looked around nervously, but there was no more sign of the undead.

"Look here," said Jacob. He pointed at a disordered line of shallow dimples in the sand, crossing and re-crossing a small but steep drift. "Someone's footsteps."

"They must be fresh. The wind would've covered them if they'd been here long." Rings followed the steps to a gaping dark archway in the stone building ahead. By one side of the door a crude chalk mark caught his eye. "We're on the right track. That's Belgin's mark."

Jacob glanced around and then ducked his head to descend the narrow steps beyond. Rings followed carefully, axe at the ready. At the bottom, the steps opened out into a long, low chamber lined with stout columns. Moving slowly, the two fighters advanced into the chamber, examining their surroundings. "I think these are more portals," Jacob said after a long moment.

"Looks like it," Rings answered. "I guess the old Netherese had an aversion to using their legs. There must be dozens of these things."

About halfway across the chamber from the stairway, they found an archway marked with a chalk symbol and a set of dwarven runes beneath it. Rings studied the archway in silence for a long time, ignoring the fighter beside him.

"Well? What is it?" Jacob asked irritably.

"Belgin and Miltiades went this way, chasing Eidola."

"What's the rest of the writing?"

"The word to open the gate," Rings said. "Are you ready?"

Jacob's eyes were far away. Rings almost repeated his question before the Tyrian absently nodded. "Go ahead."

Rings turned back to the portal and spoke the word Belgin had marked for him. Before his eyes, the gray stone seemed to shimmer and vanish, replaced by a curtain of seamless black. "It's open," he said, glancing back at Jacob.

He was just in time to see the fighter's blade punch into his chest.

Rings grunted with the impact, blinking in disbelief. Steel grated on bone as Jacob withdrew his sword, red for almost a foot of its length. Rings tried to raise the axe of his fathers to strike at his slayer, but the weapon seemed impossibly heavy, and it slipped from his grasp to fall ringing to the floor. "You bastard," he gasped once, and then the breath fled from him. With a groan he toppled to the cold stone floor, blood fountaining from his wound.

Jacob raised his sword again and met his eyes. The curly-haired fighter smiled coldly. "Thanks for reading the trigger. I don't know a word of Dwarvish. Why don't you stay here and take a breather, and I'll go on ahead and see how Miltiades and Belgin are faring."

"Why?" rasped Rings. Weakly he pushed himself up with one hand on the floor, the other clamped over the ghastly injury.

"Let's just say that Eidola's an old friend." Jacob eyed him clinically, then lowered his sword. With brutal efficiency he lashed out with one boot and kicked Rings's supporting arm out from under him, crumpling the dwarf to the floor again, then kicked him hard five times for good measure before he stopped. "Damn. You got blood all over my boot," he remarked.

Then he stepped over the small, still form and ducked into the portal.

* * * * *

Blackness and cold, an instant of silence that seared Belgin's senses, and he was through the portal again. Shivering, he swept his flank with his rapier, ready for any threat. They stood in a chamber that might have been a Netherese crypt ages ago, but it had been plundered and looted decades or centuries in the past. What was so important, so dangerous, that these dead princes were buried thousands of miles from their home? the sharper wondered. The colorful murals had flaked and peeled from exposure to the outside air, and what little statuary remained had been smashed and vandalized. The stone sepulchre in the center of the room lay broken and empty, and the doors at the far end of the chamber were torn from their hinges.

Miltiades stood beside him, scanning his side of the room. His hammer still retained his spell of illumination, and its soft silver glow cast gray shadows against the ruined walls and broken vaulting. "I'd guess that these places were built to house liches through the dark ages of undeath," he said quietly.

"Liches?" Belgin recoiled a step, even though he could plainly see that no such creature had inhabited this particular tomb for long years. "Why do you say that?"

"Netheril's archmages ruled that land. Knowing that the time of their natural deaths were upon them, maybe they arranged for the construction of tombs that would keep out looters and defilers and hide them from their living rivals but allow them to leave when they so chose."

"The Netherese were in the habit of deifying their rulers," Belgin said. "It would make sense. The desert temple was the center of a cult of death priests who watched over their lords' sleep and awaited the day of their undead resurrection. I wonder how many of these places still exist?"

"Does it matter?" Miltiades asked. "You're not thinking of using the portals to rummage through Netherese crypts, are you?"

Belgin thought of the cold emerald fire dancing in the eyes of the desert temple's dead warriors and the horrifying determination of the creature that guarded the place against intrusion. *There are easier ways to make a living,* he said to himself. *Like hunting down doppelgangers.*

"It might be handy to know where all those portals go, but I don't think I want to cross any more liches than I have to. I'll leave their tombs in peace from now on."

He laughed at his own remark, but the thick dust and rot in the chamber got into his lungs, and he coughed until it felt like someone had stabbed him between the ribs. Gasping for air, he wiped his mouth with the back of his hand and tried not to notice the dark bloody smear on his glove.

Miltiades waited, frowning. "Can you continue?"

"I'll live—for now, anyway. Lead the way."

The paladin grimaced and clapped one mailed hand to the sharper's shoulder, then turned and picked his way from the wreckage of the crypt. The ancient doors had stood at the end of a long corridor much like the one under Aetheric's palace, and a faint set of tracks marred the dust on the stone flagstones.

"No hard decisions yet," Miltiades observed, advancing down the hall. "She must have gone this way."

The passageway led several hundred feet before opening high in a dank and lightless cavern whose sides stretched away into the darkness. A cold, foul wind sighed through the chamber, hinting at vast gulfs and trackless mazes in the endless night. *What kind of place is this? It must go on forever,* Belgin thought. *I can feel* eyes in the darkness. Beneath them, a narrow ledge circled the upper portion of the cavern, with a steep scramble through a forest of stalagmites to the cavern floor. They dropped lightly from the mouth of the finished passage to the shelf of natural stone, peering down at the yawning darkness below. "How big is this place?" Belgin muttered.

"No one knows of a larger or more dangerous maze," Miltiades said. "Undermountain stretches for miles beneath the city and Mount Waterdeep. You wouldn't believe some of the things that inhabit Haalvar's dungeons, Belgin; keep your eyes open and watch your back down here."

"I really wish you'd kept that to yourself." The sharper glanced left and right, then slid down the slope to the cavern floor. He could sense water nearby, a lot of it; the wind was cold and damp, and the sound of the air seemed to indicate an immense cavern. At the bottom, a shelf of gray stone held a couple of muddy footprints. Carefully, he knelt to examine them. A few grains of wet sand remained in the tracks. "Stay toward the right," he said quietly. "I think she's following that wall."

"All right," agreed the paladin. He moved off into the darkness, keeping the dank cavern wall close by his right hand. Ahead, the sound of water grew louder, and Belgin became aware of a strong salty reek to the air. After a lifetime of piracy on the open main, he knew the smell of the sea. They followed the cavern wall until it met a dark, lapping arm of water a hundred yards or so from the passageway they'd come from. "Where did she go from here, Belgin? Can you tell?"

"Look here," the sharper said. Smooth, dark pebbles made up the shoreline, but a shallow groove showed where some of the pebbles had been displaced. "There was a boat here."

"Eidola took it?"

"I couldn't swear to it, Miltiades. It's almost impossible to track over stone, and she might have turned out away from the wall before she came here. The boat that made this mark might have been here minutes past, or it might have only landed once years ago." He stood and peered out over the Stygian lake. "Can you dim your magical light?"

"Of course," the paladin said. He lowered the hammer and allowed the silver light to fade.

As Belgin's eyes adjusted to the darkness, he became aware of a strange glimmer far off across the water. Phosphorescent green seemed to swirl and dance beneath the surface of the water, but beyond that a sickly yellow glow seemed to illuminate the far end of the cavern. "I think that's lantern light over there," he said. "Do you know where we are, Miltiades?"

The paladin nodded in the darkness beside him. "Yes, I think I do. It's Skullport."

"Skullport? What's that supposed to mean?"

"Trouble." Miltiades glowered across the underwater channel, his face unreadable in the gloom. "That's where Eidola must be."

"How do you know?" asked Belgin.

"If there's anyplace in the world she can lose us, that will be it. Come on, we'd better find another boat." The paladin led the way as they started up the shoreline, scrambling and slipping on the wet rocks. They'd only gone a few dozen paces when Belgin suddenly lunged forward to catch the paladin's arm, motioning him to silence. "What is it?"

"Something's coming up behind us," the sharper whispered. As they stood in silence for a moment, the clatter of rocks and scrape of awkward footsteps in the darkness behind them was obvious. Belgin quietly moved out away from the shore into the center of the cavern, seeking to flank their pursuer. Behind him, he sensed Miltiades steeling himself for a fight. With a whispered prayer to Tyr, the paladin brightened his hammer to the fullest power of the spell, flooding the cavern with silver light.

"Who goes there?" he called in challenge.

"Miltiades? Is that you?" Stumbling out of the darkness, Jacob blundered into the light, shielding his eyes with his hand. The fighter held his sword at the ready, and his armor showed battle damage and sand scratches from the desert storm. "I never thought I'd see you again!"

"Jacob?" Miltiades clasped the fighter's arm. "I'm sorry we left you behind, but I'm glad to see you now."

"I understand; the quest comes first. You did the right thing, Miltiades. What happened to you after the storm hit?"

"We waited for you, but—"

"One moment," said Belgin, advancing out of the darkness. "Where is Rings?"

The fighter stood silent for a long moment, and then said flatly, "He didn't make it, sharper. He died in the city."

Belgin closed his eyes and sat down heavily on the cold stones. *Kurthe, Brindra, Anvil, now Rings. Will any of us be left by the time this is all done? Any of us?* The paladins watched him, but they kept their distance. They'd traveled with Rings only a few hours, and they didn't presume to offer any platitudes for Belgin. It would have been ridiculous. *Of all of them, why is it that I'm the one still standing?* the sharper thought bitterly. *How much longer do I have, anyway? A month? Six months? But I'm alive, and they're all dead.*

All dead.

Chapter 5
Betrayal

"I hate this place," Miltiades muttered beneath a heavy cowl. Eyes narrowed at the mindless dead who milled and trudged past them in the warrenlike streets, the paladin clutched his dark cloak closer to his breast and shifted the hammer in his hand. "When I've finished with the doppelganger, I've a mind to muster a dozen or so of Tyr's bravest sons and return to set this wrong aright. It is an abomination in the eyes of the just."

Good luck, thought Belgin, but he kept his remark to himself. Skullport rambled and twisted in the darkness of the great sea cavern, illuminated by sickly yellow lanterns and green fox fire. Its dismal alleyways and ramshackle buildings reminded him of the worst pirate dens he'd seen in the Five Kingdoms, but this place was far more sinister than the rough-and-tumble seaports he knew. Skullport was a place of dark pleasures and grim designs, a place where things that could not abide the light of day chose to do their business.

"I don't like it much, either," Belgin admitted. "Best we do what we came to do and get out of here fast."

Miltiades's hood nodded. The paladin didn't care for Belgin's suggestion of a disguise, but he'd reluctantly agreed after the sharper had pointedly asked how many other paladins in shining armor he saw stomping around in Skullport's streets. "She must have friends here. I've heard that the so-called Unseen lurk somewhere in this dismal pit. We'll start with them."

"Any idea of how to find them, Miltiades? They must be called the Unseen for some reason, after all," Jacob pointed out.

The big fighter brought up the rear of their small party, keeping a sharp eye out behind them. In order to conceal their Tyrian armor, both Jacob and Miltiades had borrowed dark cloaks from ally drunks who'd never need them again. While Miltiades steamed and stewed in his shroud, Jacob grinned ear to ear, obviously enjoying the stealthy approach.

"Question one of these wretched villains scurrying by," Miltiades said. "Noph's lasso ought to elicit the answers we need. Sooner or later, we'll find one who knows something."

Belgin rolled his eyes, but assented. "Fine. It lacks subtlety, but we'll try it your way. I suspect that flashing gold in one of these alehouses would only mark us as targets, anyway." He eased the rope into his hand and measured it carefully. Together, the three men waited in the mouth of a dark alleyway, watching the mindless dead come and go. Dozens of humans, drow, and more monstrous creatures passed while they watched, but almost all traveled in pairs or small groups, watching the streets carefully. Two times the three men lassoed solitary corsairs when no one else seemed to be paying attention, but the fellows they caught knew nothing of Skullport's Unseen. Jacob whistled merrily and bound them in the filth-strewn alleyway, out of sight of the street.

After a half-hour or so, a proud mageling sauntered down the street at a moment when no one else seemed to be near. At a nod from Miltiades, Belgin threw the lasso at her without a word. The braid seemed to leap out of his hand, directing itself into a tight loop as it settled silently over the mark. "Come here, and do not resist!" Belgin hissed. The mage stiffened and started to raise her hands, but the magic of the lasso trapped her.

Snarling in rage, she plodded toward the alleyway. "You have no idea who you're trifling with, fool! When I get free—"

"You will remain silent and answer only the questions I put to you," Belgin said. The fox-faced woman broke off abruptly, but her eyes were daggers of ice. "Have you ever heard of the Unseen?"

"Yes," the mage grated angrily.

"Do you know where they can be found?"

"No."

"Feel free to respond in something besides monosyllables," Belgin said wryly. "Do you know of any way we could find them?"

"Yes."

Miltiades snorted. "So how can we find them? What's the best way?"

Struggling to resist, the mage winced and tried to mumble. The lasso of truth dragged her words forth. "There is an alehouse called the Broken Pike, several hundred yards up the street. In the back room, a man named Marks buys and sells stolen baubles. He only pretends to be a fence, though; in truth he is a doppelganger who keeps his ear to the corsairs' tales. I know that he reports to others. Apply this damned lasso to him, and he'll have to lead you to the Unseen."

"How do you know this?" Belgin asked suspiciously.

The woman glared at him. "I've used my magic on their behalf from time to time. Marks is the man I dealt with, and he paid me well."

"Are you a doppelganger, too?"

"No," she grated.

Belgin looked at Miltiades and set one hand to his knife hilt. The paladin shook his head and quickly struck the mageling with one blow of his hammer, knocking her out. She crumpled to the ground, and the sharper released the lasso's hold, coiling it in his hands.

"Do you believe her?" Jacob asked warily.

"So far Noph's lasso has proved impervious to deceit," Miltiades said.

Belgin nudged the unconscious sorceress with his toe. "What about her? She seems a bad enemy to leave on our trail."

"Doubtless she has committed many crimes, but she aided us in her quest. It would be unjust to reward her with death." Miltiades hid his hammer under his cloak, and turned into the narrow street. "Come, we've wasted enough time. Every minute we delay increases Eidola's chances of escaping us altogether."

* * * * *

The streets of Skullport were silent and almost deserted. From time to time a zombie or skeleton would stagger past, engaged on some dark mission that kept its dead limbs moving, but the deeper Belgin followed Miltiades into Skullport, the fewer people he saw. Leaning out over the alleyway, the ramshackle buildings on either side narrowed the space overhead to a mere arm's length, enclosing them in a dank tunnel of shuttered windows and sagging porches. Thin, black mire oozed around their feet as they slogged from one dim circle of lantern light to the next.

"I don't like the feel of this place," Belgin said softly. "Something's wrong here."

"It took you this long to figure that out?" Jacob snapped.

"Peace, Jacob. Belgin is right," Miltiades said. He slowed and stopped, searching the street with his piercing gaze. In the flickering light of the next lamp, a ramshackle old building boasted a faded sign marked by a rusty polearm, maybe twenty paces ahead. The paladin frowned and tightened his grip on his warhammer. "The Broken Pike is just ahead. Come on."

Belgin followed, but as he glanced down at the ground to pick out his steps, he noticed a soft silver shadow dancing and moving across the dark mud and rotted wood. At the same time, a gelid malaise settled over him, his bones aching with preternatural cold. *It's behind me,* he realized as the dancing shadows grew darker, more sharply defined. Mouth dry, he turned like a sleepwalker to gaze on the thing that stalked him.

A grinning skull hovered in the air behind him, limned by a cold silver fire. Everything its argent flames illuminated seemed to acquire a faint dusting of hateful frost, boards splitting from the sudden cold, black mire frosting over in a filthy rime of ice. "Miltiades!" Belgin gasped in horror, recoiling from the apparition. He stumbled and fell, scrabbling backwards through the freezing muck as the silent skull approached. Beside him, Jacob whirled and shrank away in fear, backing into a dark alleyway. The thing ignored him and continued.

Sensing the cold and the wrong, Miltiades whirled to confront the creature, shedding his black cloak with one swift motion. "Stay your approach, creature of evil!" he barked, holding his hammer forward. "Leave us be! You have no power over the just."

"Miltiades of Tyr," the skull sang, its voice as thin and hateful as the keening of a banshee. "You have interfered with the dead of Skullport. Now you must pay for your disobedience."

"Miltiades! What's it talking about? What does it want?" Belgin gasped.

"I defied the spirits that hold this place in thrall the last time I visited," Miltiades rasped. "It seems that they've been waiting for my return."

With two swift bounds he closed with the silver death's-head and struck it with his hammer, but the weapon seemed to glance from the thing with little effect. From the blank eye sockets two sickly green rays sprang forth, blasting Miltiades back against the right-hand building with bone-jarring force. The paladin fell in a clatter of armor.

Howling, Jacob sliced at the thing with his sword but missed. Belgin attacked with his rapier, but the narrow point seemed to slide off the old bone like a pat of butter skittering across a hot pan. The skull ignored them both and struck at Miltiades again with the twin emerald rays, pummelling the holy warrior as he tried to find his feet.

"I can't stop this thing!" the sharper cried.

Beside him, Jacob backed up a couple of steps, glancing around. "More trouble coming up the alley," he announced. "I'll handle it." The curly-haired fighter abandoned the floating skull and dashed back the way they'd come.

Belgin tried to stab the creature again, but his rapier glided away under the influence of some magical force each time he struck at the skull. He risked one quick glance down the street. *Whatever's down there, Jacob had better handle it. I've got my hands full here.* He saw nothing but impenetrable shadows and ruined buildings in that direction, and before he could make out what Jacob was up to, the skull thing turned on him.

"Sentence has been passed on Miltiades of Tyr. Do not interfere," it stated coldly.

Belgin stared, frozen to the spot by the creature's black gaze. Nearby, Miltiades groaned and pushed himself to his feet. The skull's jaws gaped open as if in laughter, and it turned away from the sharper to finish off the paladin. *I've got to do something! Wait . . . the building. That might work!* The silver skull drifted beneath the overhanging porch to peer down at the paladin, almost as if it had a spectral foot to set on Miltiades's neck. For a moment, it drifted just underneath the rotten roof timbers of the building's porch. With desperate strength, Belgin whirled and kicked hard at a rotten post, cracking it. A second kick knocked it free.

In a roaring crash of wood and debris, the porch collapsed, burying the skull under an avalanche of old timber. Belgin reeled back from the destruction, coughing from the dust and mold until his legs gave out. In between wracking gasps, he noticed Miltiades standing unsteadily, one hand clamped over a streaming wound in his side. The paladin picked his way over toward the sharper, hauling him upright.

"Where's Jacob?" Miltiades said. "We need to get off this street."

"He saw something behind us ," Belgin rasped, but the act of speaking sent him into another paroxysm of coughing. When he looked up again, wiping his mouth, a pair of new silver skulls approached, these glowing with an azure blaze.

"Belgin of Edenvale, you have interfered with the dead of Skullport," one began. Its companion spoke in chorus: "Miltiades of Tyr—"

From the alley mouth beside them, a brilliant bolt of lightning stabbed forth, forking to impale both guardians on white skewers of energy. In the blink of an eye both were blasted to shards in a rolling thunderclap that left Belgin's ears ringing and his eyes dancing with spots. "What now?" he groaned.

Miltiades shook his head. "I know not." Grimacing in pain, he straightened and faced the darkness, hammer held lightly in one hand. His silver armor gleamed like a brand of faith in the stinking mire and rot of the dismal street. "Who goes there? Show yourself!"

"I should have expected you to start a war with the powers of Skullport the moment you returned, Miltiades," a woman's voice replied. Stepping into the light, a tall woman of exquisite beauty and iron determination appeared, tapping a slender wand in her hand. Despite himself, Belgin blinked in astonishment. It wasn't every day that he was rescued from certain death by beautiful women. "Come quickly. We must move fast to elude more of the skull guardians," she said.

Belgin gathered up what dignity he could and looked to Miltiades. "You know her?"

The paladin simply nodded. "She is Aleena Paladinstar." His eyes darkened. "A friend, but one who has much to answer for."

"Good," said the sharper. "I'd get bored if anything ever became easy or obvious." He began a sweeping bow to the lady before him, but as he moved tearing pain lanced through his chest. Gasping in surprise at the bright blood that fumed from his mouth, Belgin collapsed in the street, darkness whirling in to blanket him.

* * * * *

Silver light danced above him, cool, supernal. He felt light as a feather, almost as if he'd slipped free of some heavy shackle. I'm dying, he realized. He didn't feel much fear, only a little sadness. It wasn't as if he hadn't been expecting it, after all. That was the manner of the blood-forge's curse—you could be fine all day long, only to keel over dead at sunset. Belgin had seen it often enough. If he'd had the strength, he would have laughed until he cried. All the heartache, all the trouble, of the *Kissing Shark*'s last voyage and Entreri's damned contract, and I was going to kick off anyway. There must have been a better way to spend my last days.

"He's fading fast." A woman's voice, distant and concerned. "Cure the affliction quickly, or we'll lose him."

"I know, I know. But it's not a mundane disease. It's a magical curse, the effect of growing up in a land ruled by a bloodforge."

"If I counter the curse, can you then heal him?"

"Tyr willing, I think so."

Motion now, someone dumping him unceremoniously on a rickety wooden table. Belgin gazed up at the smoke-stained roof-beams of a tavern, impossibly far away. *What better place for me to die than in some dismal alehouse? Irony on irony. I'm almost sorry I won't see how this turns out.* The woman spoke words he knew, working a potent spell designed to undo curses. He wanted to tell her to save her magic, that the priests of Edenvale had tried that measure long ago, but he couldn't find his breath. Then Miltiades spoke loudly, calling on the power of his god, as his hands descended to rest on Belgin's chest.

Silver lightning jolted his chest, although his eyes saw

nothing but a soft glow. The sharper gasped and bounced from the table in reaction, then drew a great cold breath that seemed to go on forever. It had been years since he could hold so much air in his lungs. Flinching, he waited for the inevitable fit to rack him again . . . but this time, it didn't come.

"Belgin? Can you hear me?" Beside him, Miltiades helped him to sit upright. Taut with worry, the paladin peered into his face. "Speak, man! Tyr's power has made you whole again."

"I can breathe," Belgin whispered. He couldn't believe it. He felt weak as a kitten, drained and exhausted, but with some hidden sense he could feel that the wreckage that had cluttered his lungs and stolen his wind for so many months was gone. He sucked in another great gasp of air just to enjoy the sensation. "Miltiades, what did you do?"

"Not I, but Tyr," the paladin answered. He stood and smiled. "The bloodforge disease that ravaged you could not be defeated by magical healing nor undone by simply removing the curse. But both spells together succeeded where either one alone would have failed. Through me, Tyr cured the disease, but only after Aleena here defeated the curse."

The sharper looked from the paladin to the mage and back again. Beyond the two, he became aware of more details of the room beyond. It was the common room of a squalid alehouse, dank and smoky, so small that the three of them seemed to crowd the place. The front door was barred, and in the opposite corner a pair of villainous-looking pirates sprawled, dead or asleep. By the filthy ale tap, a small, mouselike man sat against the wall, bound by the lasso.

"Where are we?" asked Belgin.

"The Broken Pike," answered Miltiades. "We carried you here after you collapsed. Aleena and I had to secure the premises before turning our attention to you." He grimaced. "It's fortunate that we acted when we did. You were on the verge of death."

"Fortunate, indeed," the sharper breathed. "Is that

Marks in the lasso?"

The paladin nodded. "He wasn't inclined to offer us the hospitality of his establishment, so we decided to give him a chance to reconsider." He glanced across the table at Aleena. "Perhaps when we've finished with Marks, we'll find another use for the lasso of truth. What do you think, Aleena?"

Under the paladin's ire, most men would have flinched, but Aleena simply met his gaze with determination. "I have nothing to hide, Miltiades."

"Fine. Then maybe you'd care to explain why you destroyed the portal and stranded us in the Utter East. Or why we were sent to rescue a monster, not a high lady. Or for that matter why I shouldn't suspect you of being a doppelganger yourself."

Aleena folded her arms and met the paladin's anger with misdirection. "You've learned that Eidola is a doppelganger then? How did you find out?"

"It might have been when she took a crocodile's shape and killed Noph," Belgin said. "Or when she turned into a great black mastiff and ran off through the dungeons of Doegan, or perhaps when she turned into a horrible fiend and commanded a trio of vrock to attack us. Somewhere along the way we figured it out."

The sorceress directed a fierce glare at him, but Belgin only laughed. "Wasn't she wearing a girdle? A large belt, chased with gold and silver?"

"No," Miltiades said. "We never saw any such thing."

"Damn," Aleena sighed. "Someone must have removed it for her."

"Removed what?" Belgin asked.

"The girdle was a magical bond that locked Eidola into her human shape and personality. As long as she wore it, she could work no evil. If she wears it no longer, there's no telling where she could go or what she could do." She frowned, thinking. "You'd better tell me what happened after you arrived in Doegan."

Miltiades started to answer, but Belgin broke in abruptly. "Oh, no. You won't throw us off the scent that easily, my lady. Before Miltiades tells you what he was doing in the Five Kingdoms, maybe you should explain how you knew of this girdle that Eidola should have been wearing. And how you knew that she was a doppelganger." In one fluid motion, he drew his rapier and set the point in the hollow of Aleena's throat. "We've good reason to be suspicious of foes who look like friends these days."

Eyes blazing, Aleena flushed and began to raise her hands. A gentle shake of the sharper's head persuaded her to hold still. "Miltiades, tell this fool to lower his blade," she grated.

The paladin looked at her thoughtfully. "Not yet, Aleena. Answer his question."

"The Blackstaff and I have known of Eidola's true nature for several months now," she said, glaring at Belgin over the shining blade of the rapier. "We keep a close eye on anyone who gets close to Piergeiron, and we spotted her as soon as she made her move against the Open Lord."

"Why didn't you stop her then?" Miltiades demanded. "What kind of game were you playing with your father's life, girl?"

"We didn't strike at her because she possesses a hold of some kind on my father's mind, perhaps even his very soul. We feared that slaying her would kill the Open Lord, too. And if she does hold his soul in her hands, my father would not only be dead but destroyed utterly. We couldn't take the chance." A hint of uncertainty flickered across her proud, confident features. "Khelben and I decided that we had to render Eidola harmless if we couldn't move against her openly. The Blackstaff crafted a girdle of righteousness to bind Eidola. It prevented her from working harm against the Open Lord, or anyone else for that matter, and held her in the shape she currently wore. She couldn't have removed it herself."

"You could have informed me of this before sending me to the Utter East," Miltiades growled.

"Khelben and I hoped that you'd be able to retrieve Eidola with the girdle still binding her. We should have realized that she'd find a way to remove it once she was out of our sight long enough."

"What's the nature of the hold Eidola possesses over this Piergeiron fellow?" Belgin asked.

"I don't know how she did it, but I think that Eidola trapped some portion of his soul within the prison of a soul gem," Aleena answered. "It shouldn't be possible. These devices wrest the victim's soul from his body altogether, destroying him utterly. But Khelben and I can think of no other enchantment that might allow Eidola to hold my father's life in her hands." She gently reached up to push Belgin's rapier from her neck. "Miltiades, every minute we waste places my father in greater danger. Please, we have to catch her quickly."

Belgin looked at the paladin. "Are you satisfied, Miltiades?"

The paladin nodded. "Almost, Belgin. Lower your sword."

With a flourish, Belgin returned his rapier to its scabbard. "My apologies, Lady Aleena. I—" His words were cut off by a sudden icy chill that settled over his limbs, rendering him motionless. A spell of holding! he realized with horror.

The sorceress whispered and gestured, finishing her enchantment. "As long as we're demanding explanations, Miltiades, I thought your companion had a few to offer."

The paladin turned his attention from Aleena to Belgin, the same measuring gaze in his eyes. He held up a silver chain, with a pendant in the shape of a harp suspended from it. "We found this beneath your shirt as we worked to save your life. What business do the Harpers have here, Belgin?"

Belgin's heart sank. He cleared his throat awkwardly but found he could still speak. "I'm no Harper, Miltiades."

"Then why do you wear the pin?" Aleena demanded. "Do you make a habit of impersonating Harpers for your own purposes?"

"I've seen you wield magic, read runes more ancient than any I've ever seen, and track with the skill of a Silverymoon ranger," Miltiades said. "You're no ordinary scoundrel, Belgin, no matter how much you try to pass yourself off as one. You're a bard, and a skillful one. And you wear the Harp. So how did you come to be in the Utter East, Harper? Did you travel with Entreri, perhaps?"

"Miltiades, we don't have time for this," Belgin grated. "Eidola is—"

"I know about Eidola," the paladin interrupted. "I'm tired of deceptions. Tell me who you really are and what you're doing here."

Belgin closed his eyes and sighed. "Hundreds of years ago, when the Ffolk first came to the lands that would become the Five Kingdoms, there was a bard named Dereth Caelwindar among them. He was one who wore the Harp in the Moonshaes, and he followed the Ffolk to the Utter East and settled in Edenvale. Learning that he was thousands of miles from his brothers and sisters, he decided to continue the tradition as best he could. When he felt his years gaining on him, he selected a young lass to learn the ways of the Harp. Generation after generation, each Harper passed his lore and knowledge to an apprentice, keeping the tradition alive."

"Amazing," breathed Aleena. "Who could have known?"

"Almost twenty years ago, Lady Jaele Serwid chose me to carry on in her footsteps," Belgin continued. He attempted a wry smile. "I fear that I was not much of student. I was certain I had better things to do than carry a torch for a secret brotherhood centuries dead, and I was always quicker to look out for myself than for others around me. I might carry the Harp, Miltiades, but I've never been a Harper."

The paladin studied him a moment longer, and then nodded. "He speaks the truth, Aleena. You may release him."

The cold shackles holding him seemed to fade away, leaving nothing but a memory of immobility. Shivering, Belgin rubbed his arms and stamped his feet. Miltiades offered him the silver pendant again, but Belgin shook his head. "No, you were right. I have no right to wear it."

The paladin pressed the Harp into his hand. "There's

more to you than you think, Belgin. I've known more than one Harper in my day. Whatever you've been, whatever you've done, you've earned the Harp as much as anyone I've ever met. Wear it well."

Belgin considered a sharp answer, but to his own surprise he reached for the pendant and slipped it beneath his shirt. For all the things I've done, he thought, betrayal, murder, robbery, and cheating of all descriptions, I still can't bring myself to mock this lonely symbol. Not now. "You have a way of making me believe that I'm more than I am, paladin," he said in wonder. "Why do you do it?"

"A good man is a hammer in the hand of Tyr," Miltiades answered.

By the bar, the small man bound in the lasso of truth groaned and stirred, climbing back to consciousness. The paladin took up the end of the magical lariat and wrapped it loosely around his shield hand, keeping his hammer free for action. After a moment, the man blinked and looked up at Miltiades, towering over him.

"What's going on? Who do you think you are?" he snapped in a shrill voice. "You have no idea who you're tangling with, you arse-kissing numbskull!"

"Marks," said Miltiades wearily, "Be silent and listen to me. I have two questions for you. First, can you walk? And second, can you lead me to the lair of the Unseen?"

The man's face turned red and veins stood out on his forehead as he tried to fight the compulsion of the lasso, but the enchantment proved too strong for him. "Yes. And yes."

"Well, come on, then. It's time you were about Tyr's work, scoundrel." Miltiades reached down and hauled the small barkeep to his feet, dragging him to the door. He paused to throw a dark cloak over the man, concealing the lasso that bound him, and then opened the door to the rank street. Belgin and Aleena exchanged suspicious glances, then followed. "Lead the way," Miltiades said.

Chapter 6
Justice

Skullport yawned around them, pale fox fire dancing on an open grave. The secret city decayed with a conscious, palpable effort. Mud oozed beneath Belgin's feet. Boards and shingles in the buildings around him creaked and fell, as if something old and rotten was waking from a long slumber. The reek of the place threatened to taint his new-found health, clogging his nose and throat with a noisome miasma he could literally taste. Silent, mindless dead walked all about him, shackled to their rotting corpses by the chains of sinister necromancy. *But for Miltiades and Aleena, I'd be one more of those poor souls,* he realized. *When we're done with this, I think I'll retire to* someplace quiet and peaceful. Someplace where the dead stay in the ground and everyone is exactly who they seem to be.

"You are dead men," Marks said clearly. He marched along between Belgin and Miltiades, covered in a moth-eaten robe. The sharper held the lasso close by the man's side, concealing the fact that Marks was securely bound. "You know that, don't you? If you leave now, you might gain a few weeks, maybe a few months, to set your affairs in order. We'll find you soon enough."

"I hate waiting," Belgin said amicably. "If I'm going to be killed anyway, today's as good a day as any. Now, where next?"

"This way," the small man muttered, scuffing his feet in the mud. He shuffled ahead, glaring fiercely at the humans who followed him. They only traveled a few hundred yards as the bat flew, but no street in the hidden city ran straight for more than twenty paces at a time. They twisted and turned through alleys and courts, along streets and over rickety wharves, turning again and again.

"Are you taking us to the Unseen by the most direct route?" Aleena asked archly.

"Yes," snarled Marks. "You'll regret—"

"Shut up," Belgin advised. The man fell silent, fuming and helpless. The sharper looked over the short scoundrel at Miltiades, striding along with unswerving determination. "Miltiades, do you have any plan of action when we find these creatures?"

"Smite them," the paladin answered. "Attack directly, with justice and righteousness on our side. Hit them hard."

"You'd make a lousy pirate," Belgin muttered. He scratched at his jaw, considering his next approach. "What if there are a lot of them? I mean, more than you can smite?"

The paladin looked over at him. "There are never too many," he said softly.

The sharper paused a long moment. "Right," he said thoughtfully. "Lady Aleena, perhaps you have some stratagem in mind?"

The Waterdhavian shook her head and met Belgin's gaze with a condescending sniff. "I'm working on it. I think I can come up with—wait, someone comes."

She broke off and drew Belgin and Miltiades toward a reeking derelict of a building, sheltering in the shadows of its overhanging upper stories. The bard tapped Marks softly on the shoulder and shook his head, cautioning the prisoner to silence.

From the gloom ahead of them, a familiar figure in shining silver armor appeared, flanked by a brawny youth in golden scale mail and a seasoned old warrior carrying a long quarterstaff. Miltiades started in disbelief. "It's Jacob! With Kern and Trandon!"

"Ho there, Miltiades!" Jacob called. With a quick sweep of his eyes, he surveyed the street, searching for threats. Satisfied, he turned toward their place of concealment. "You'll never believe who I found wandering around in this forsaken hole!"

"Kern! Trandon! What are you doing here? Where are the others?" Miltiades said, stepping forward to greet them. "Did you succeed in foiling Entreri's designs?"

Kern smiled. He looked a little tired, but cheered by the sight of his friend and mentor. "Well, we followed you after we finished our business in Doegan. Entreri and Noph are dead. The others chose to remain in Doegan to fight off the fiends."

"You destroyed the bloodforge, then?" Belgin asked.

Kern glanced at Trandon, then nodded. "Yes," he answered. "We thought we'd come after you as quickly as we could to help you track down Eidola."

"I should've known we'd end up here again," Trandon remarked.

"Where did you find them, Jacob?" Miltiades asked.

"Yes, where did you find them?" Belgin added. "And what drew you away from the fight with the skull guardians? Those things almost killed us."

Jacob trotted closer. "What's the plan, Miltiades? Is this Marks?"

He pointed past Miltiades at the small man bound in

the lasso. The paladin turned at his gesture, looking over his shoulder at the prisoner who stood behind him. Jacob's grin faded and his eyes went dark as cold coals. In the space of a single step his great sword appeared in his hand, almost as if it were a part of him.

Betrayal, Belgin realized. "Look out!" he howled.

As Miltiades wheeled to confront the threat, Jacob struck. Betrayed and deceived, somehow the paladin almost deflected the attack from his flank, flinging out his hammer in a desperate parry. Jacob's blow smashed the warhammer from Miltiades's hands and hacked through his shining breastplate. Miltiades grunted and fell spinning to the ground, blood streaming from the horrible rent over his left shoulder. "Jacob!" he cried.

Without thought Belgin leaped to help the stricken paladin, but Kern was too close to him. With the speed of striking snake the smiling red-haired youth reached out with a hand that became a swordlike blade of bone.

"Now, now," he said, hissing in mockery.

Somehow Belgin twisted out of the stroke, taking a long, jagged cut across his scalp but keeping his head on his shoulders. White spots starred his vision. He stumbled and fell backwards to the rotten boardwalk, blinking. Doppelgangers. Of course.

Aleena began to work some kind of spell, but the Trandon-duplicate turned on her. With one brutal stroke he clubbed the graceful noblewoman to the ground with a forearm that had grown into a spiked mace. Aleena's half-formed spell burst in a shower of fiery sparks, hissing and sizzling in the dark mire of the street.

Marks howled as an ember struck him, then hopped away, hobbled by the lasso around his torso. Belgin caught the end of the rope and yanked Marks off his feet as he rolled away from Kern's attack. "Stick around," he muttered. The Kern-thing smashed its murderous blade down at the bard, but Belgin scrambled back and somehow found his feet.

In the street, Miltiades rose to his knees, groping for his warhammer. "When did you take Jacob?" he rasped. "When?"

"I haven't been Jacob in a long time, human fool," the blond-haired fighter replied. He raised his sword for the killing stroke. Miltiades, wounded and unarmed, raised his hand to ward off the blow.

From the darkness behind Jacob a gleam of silver drifted through the air, tumbling slowly before it crashed into the fighter with the shrill ring of metal meeting metal. What now? Belgin wasted a precious moment gaping at the scene in front of him before a flurry of violent slashes and stabs from the Kern-doppelganger sent him scrabbling and squirming backwards, narrowly avoiding an ugly death. "Bastard!" he swore angrily. He finally found the rapier at his belt and drew the blade in time to drive the false Kern back a step or two.

Behind the Kern-doppelganger, Jacob reeled drunkenly and stumbled away from Miltiades. A dwarven fighting axe lodged in the side of the fighter's head. Amazingly, the creature reached up and wrenched the gory blade from his skull. Then a small, stocky shape barreled into his legs, taking him down.

"Stab me when I'm not looking, will you?" shouted Rings. "Leave me to die in a stinking desert, eh? By Moradin's beard, I'll teach you better, you traitorous wretch!" The dwarf found his axe with one hand and set to work, slamming the heavy blade into Jacob over and over again.

Belgin danced back a step as the false Kern slid to one side, warily eyeing the new threat. The Trandon-doppelganger joined him, pressing Belgin with massive blows that split boards and splintered anything in their path.

"Come on! We can still get them!" he hissed to his comrade in arms.

"Not if I cheat," Belgin said. He raised one hand and spoke an old spell, one of the few he knew that was any good in a fight. From his hand, a green arrowhead of energy streaked out to strike the Trandon-doppelganger in its chest. The bolt of energy slagged at once into a vitriolic patch that seethed and bubbled, eating its way into the creature's body. Shrieking with inhuman pain, the Trandon-thing staggered back and fell, its heels drumming against the rotten planking.

The Kern-duplicate snarled in anger and struck back, cutting a shallow gash across Belgin's left arm and another under his ribs. The sharper riposted, running the doppelganger through its midsection with his rapier. The creature hissed and recoiled, then pressed forward again. "Fine," muttered Belgin. He danced back two steps, steadied his hand, then rammed the point of his rapier into the monster's left eye. The doppelganger collapsed like a puppet with its strings cut. Belgin panted and watched his fallen foes for signs of consciousness, his wounds stinging abominably.

No one around him was moving.

Aleena lay dazed on the ground, an ugly purple mark on her forehead. Slowly, Miltiades hauled himself to his feet. With his teeth clenched, he spoke a prayer to Tyr, and the blood coursing from his broken armor slowed to a trickle. Rings stood up as well, his axe dripping with gore. Belgin winced and sheathed his rapier.

"Good timing, Rings," the sharper said. "What happened to you? Jacob said you were dead."

The dwarf bared his teeth in a fearsome grin. "Oh, he sure thought I was. We found the portal you marked for us in the desert temple, and then that orc-kissing bastard ran me through without a word. He thought he'd killed me, alright."

"You don't look poorly for a mortally wounded dwarf," Miltiades said with a grimace of pain.

Rings smiled and tugged at a silver band that pierced his eyebrow. "I got better, as they say. Years ago I found this enchanted ring in a mage's tower. It takes time, but the dweomer repairs any injury that doesn't kill me instantly. I never needed it as badly as I did a few hours ago, that's for certain." He looked down at the creature that had imitated Jacob, sprawled beneath him in a spreading pool of blood. He snorted and kicked the motionless form, hard. "Guess you found out about him."

Aleena moaned and stirred. Miltiades limped over to

the mage and pressed one hand to her forehead, speaking a prayer. The ugly wound faded, leaving a faint mark. The woman's eyes fluttered open, a little glassy at first. "Doppelgangers," she groaned. "Watch out—"

"We dealt with them," Miltiades said. He helped Aleena to her feet. The mage swayed but quickly found her balance, and her eyes seemed to clear and focus. "You're lucky to be alive. Another inch or two, and the creature would have stove in your skull."

Aleena took in the site with one sweep of her eyes and returned her attention to Rings. "Who's he?"

"A friend whom Jacob didn't kill as thoroughly as he should have," Belgin said. He frowned, thinking. "You know, Miltiades, Jacob must have been a doppelganger all along. He turned on Rings before we returned to Skullport, so he must have been replaced before we set off in pursuit of Eidola."

The paladin crouched by the imposter's body. In death, he still resembled the blond-haired fighter he'd pretended to be; only the great blade of bone that grew from his forearm, a clever mimicry of a sword, marked him as a shapeshifter. "They must have overcome him the first time we were here," he said quietly. "I never suspected. How did he hide his evil from me? That should be impossible."

"Greater doppelgangers can do that," Aleena said quietly. "We had plenty of time to study Eidola. When she wore the Eidola's shape, she was Eidola Boraskyr. In her mind, in her thoughts, she was a perfect mimicry. If the doppelganger that replaced Jacob was one of her kind, he could defeat virtually any test that might reveal his true nature."

"He'd have killed me for certain if Rings had not intervened," Miltiades sighed. He looked up and clapped one hand to the dwarf's shoulder. "My thanks, Rings. I owe you my life."

The dwarven pirate scowled. "Don't thank me, paladin. After what he did to me, I'd have killed him if he was sipping tea with a table full of old maids." He cleaned his axe on Jacob's cloak and thrust it through the loop on his belt. "Say, who's that little rodent?"

Belgin followed his glance, only to find Marks quietly edging into a nearby alleyway. He bounded forward and caught the trailing end of the lasso with one hand. "Oh, no you don't," he said with a cold smile. "We've got places to go, Marks, and you're the fellow who's going to take us there."

* * * * *

I'm going to need a scorecard soon to keep track of the roster changes, Belgin thought absently as they followed Marks through the streets of Skullport. First there were the seven of us, the Sharkers. Then Belmer, who was actually Entreri, killed Kurthe. Brindra perished, fighting the fiends. Anvil was struck down by the doppelganger masquerading as Jacob—even though we didn't know that at the time. That pup Noph joined us, and we lost him beneath the mage-king's palace. Rings and I followed Miltiades and Jacob after Eidola . . . then we lost Rings and Jacob in the city . . . then Jacob found us, and left us again, as we found Aleena . . . and now, finally, Jacob is dead and Rings is here again. He rubbed his eyes, realizing suddenly that he couldn't remember the last time he had slept.

"I hope Eidola's having the kind of day I am," he snorted.

"If Tyr smiles on us, hers will turn out much worse," Miltiades said. He attempted to smile, but it came out poorly. Haggard with exhaustion, still pained by the wound Jacob had given him, even Miltiades was near the end of his strength. The paladin grimaced and spoke to Marks. "Well, where is it? We must be on top of the Unseen by now."

The small fence scowled angrily. "We're here. You want that warehouse." At Belgin's doubtful expression, Marks sighed and went on. "We don't have a headquarters or a fortress, you idiots. We don't need much more than a few safehouses and meeting places. You'll want the side door; the front door leads to nothing but an empty storage room."

"Is Eidola there?" Rings asked.

"There's a good chance of it," Marks said. "It's about the best place for her to go to get out of sight and rest for a time."

The four interlopers withdrew to the shadows of a dismal alley across the street from the ramshackle structure Marks had indicated. It seemed innocuous enough, one more disused old building in a town full of them. Miltiades frowned, thinking. "Anything else we should expect?"

"There's a second structure inside the first. In the space between the buildings there are two leucrotta, unchained to roam the building. They'll attack any who don't respond with the correct password. The inner door is marked by a very dangerous glyph, and the room beyond is guarded, usually by four or five doppelgangers in human guise." Marks winced and muttered, trying to resist the rope's compulsion, but he continued despite his efforts. "If there's anyone important here, expect more guards."

"Tell us the password and the name of the glyph," Aleena said.

" *'Derzhim haalva,'* " Marks replied. "The glyph is *cirr*."

The sorceress nodded. "I have no further use for this one, Miltiades."

Without ceremony, the paladin sapped the villain with a short-hafted swing of his warhammer. Marks groaned and sank to the ground. Belgin released the magical lasso from the small man and coiled it at his belt. "What happens if Eidola isn't here?" he asked quietly.

"We'll keep looking," Miltiades answered. "Come on." The paladin led them across the street and into the opposite alleyway, pausing at the door Marks had indicated. He glanced back once to make sure everyone was ready and then pulled the door open and stepped inside.

The interior of the warehouse was nearly pitch-black, littered with casks and crates stacked at odd angles. A rank, rotten smell permeated the building. Aleena quietly produced a slender wand from her sleeve and spoke a word that woke it to soft incandescence. The place was a mazelike tangle of bales and boxes, stacked to create a winding labyrinth. "The room we seek must be hidden deeper inside," she observed.

"Agreed," said Miltiades. He led the way into the rickety mass, threading between leaning stacks of barrels and kegs. Somewhere off in the darkness, beyond their soft globe of light, something large snorted and moved. "The leucrotta," whispered the paladin.

From the darkness, a high, piping voice whispered, "What do we see, eh?"

"Humans. Delicious, delectable humans," answered a second piping voice from the other side of the chamber. "Oh, how fortunate we are today!"

"Now, now, we must first see if we may devour them. They may be friends."

"Perhaps. But who would know if we didn't tell, eh? Eh?"

"We shall be punished if we are caught," admonished the first voice. "No, we must ask to see if they know the password. Do you, delectable humans? Do you know the words?"

"Please, say that you don't," said the second voice.

"*Derzhim haalva*," snapped Aleena. "Now, leave us be. We have business here."

Silence greeted them. After a long moment, Belgin whispered, "Did they agree?"

"They're not attacking us," Aleena offered.

Keeping a wary eye on the clutter and darkness around them, they picked their way up to a door in the room's far wall. There Aleena quietly disarmed the glyph Marks had warned them of. With one more nervous glance at the darkness behind them, she said, "We can enter any time you're ready. Do we have any reason to think there may be friends within?"

"No, not that I know of," Miltiades said.

"Good." The mage raised her hand and spoke a soft word. An azure nimbus of light sprang into being around each of them, flickering and leaping.

"Aleena! This spell is intended to make someone easier

to strike!" Belgin hissed in alarm. "What do you think you're doing?"

The mage smiled grimly. "I know, bard. But if we're going to fight doppelgangers, we'll be able to tell at a glance who is with us and who isn't. The doppelgangers can mimic our faces and features to their hearts' content, but they won't be able to mimic the aura I've just created with this spell. When we step through that door, you can strike at anyone who isn't glowing."

Miltiades, Belgin, and Rings exchanged glances. They remembered what had happened the last time they cornered Eidola. "A sound idea," the paladin said. He readied his hammer and shield, then kicked the door down, leaping inside with a great battle cry: "For Tyr and justice!"

In the room beyond, half a dozen human guards—no, doppelgangers in human guise, Belgin reminded himself—sprang to their feet to meet the attack. The first died under Miltiades's hammer before he even raised his hand in his own defense, and the second fell a moment later to a hissing ray of green energy from Aleena's wand. In the space of a moment, it seemed that everything in the room changed. Three Miltiades now filled the small guardroom, along with two Aleenas and two Rings. A towering hook horror loomed behind them, screeching and clacking its claws. Only the original Miltiades, Rings, and Aleena glowed with faerie fire; their mimics were perfect, but not good enough.

"This makes things much easier," Belgin muttered. No one wasted their attention on his sarcasm. He dashed forward to engage a faux-Aleena, slashing and stabbing with his rapier.

A flash of light and a sudden sharp slap of thunder marked another of Aleena's spells as she downed three more doppelgangers at once with a bolt of lightning. Belgin hurled himself into the fray, still pursuing his original foe. As the sharper finished off his opponent, two doors burst open and more doppelgangers streamed into the room, screaming with rage. "We've got trouble!" he called to his comrades.

"We've got trouble!" echoed a false-Belgin who fell on

him with a flurry of blows. The sharper grimaced and parried his counterpart's attack. With a quick move he riposted and took his doppelganger through the heart, watching in horror as his own face grayed and contorted with mortal agony. I didn't need to see what I'd look like with a sword between my ribs, he thought grimly. Baring his teeth in determination, he returned to the fight.

The next foe he faced was Eidola.

He blinked in amazement. The doppelganger hesitated, perhaps surprised herself. "You!" she barked, her voice rough as stone. "What will it take to teach you the extent of your folly?" With a bestial roar she shifted into the monstrous form of a minotaur and smashed a colossal axe down at him, a two-handed blow that could have split a tree.

Belgin yelped and dodged back. "Eidola! She's here! The minotaur! No, the cuttlefish! No, the elf mage!" Even as he tried to dodge her attacks, avoid the other doppelgangers boiling into room, and keep track of his comrades, Eidola shifted from shape to shape in a fluid motion that kept him back on his heels. "Damn it, will you just pick one shape and stick to it!"

Eidola, now a tall, handsome elf with a cruel twist to his mouth, raised her (or his?) hands and streamed blue-glowing darts of magical energy at Belgin, Miltiades, and Aleena. The bard tried to duck aside, but one bolt struck him on the hip, jolting him with a shock that knocked him to his knees. Belgin cursed and tried to rise, but Eidola pressed her advantage, working another spell that struck at him with a lance of scorching fire. When did she learn to cast spells? he thought in disbelief. Even as the fire scorched his shirt and coat, Belgin twisted and slipped behind another doppelganger, using its body to shield him from the flame. With an agonized screech, the creature caught fire and staggered away.

Aleena replied with a powerful invocation that stabbed at Belgin's ears like a dagger of ice. From her hand, a streaming sheet of lightning flashed forward to level the room, blasting false Miltiades and duplicate Rings to ash and ruin. The Eidola-mage deflected the spell with some manner of magical shield she'd woven held against Aleena's spell. As the roaring thunder died away, Belgin realized that Eidola stood alone at the far side of the room, while he and his companions stood largely unharmed at the other. Between them lay nothing.

In the sudden silence, he stepped forward and said clearly to his comrades, "That's Eidola. She's right there."

The moment shattered. Snarling a curse, Eidola wheeled and dashed back through the doorway she'd emerged from, vanishing into the darkness. Miltiades, streaming blood from a new cut high on his forehead, let loose with a very unpaladin-like howl of rage and thundered after her, brandishing his hammer. Aleena followed, a step behind, pelting after the paladin.

Together, Belgin and Rings sprinted after Miltiades and Eidola.

* * * * *

The chamber beyond the doppelganger lair was nothing more than the topmost landing of a dark, spiralling stairway leading down. Green, rank moss coated the stone with a wet and slippery blanket. Clattering and cursing, Belgin and Rings raced recklessly down into the abyss, trailing the silver gleam and green witch fire of the paladin and the wizard. More than once, the sharper lost his footing and slipped or stumbled a few steps before steadying himself against the narrow walls.

"Does this place have no end to it?" he growled in frustration.

"The rock tells me no," Rings answered between breaths. "This maze goes much, much farther than you'd think."

The stair finally came to an end. Belgin and Rings blundered into Miltiades and Aleena, who stood in a long corridor that arrowed out of sight both left and right. The paladin and the sorceress peered each way, plainly frustrated.

"Which way?" snapped Miltiades. "She's getting

away?"

"How should I know?" Aleena replied tersely. "Be still a moment, all of you! We might hear her footsteps."

Belgin, Rings, and Miltiades froze. Aleena paused a moment, tilting her head to hear better. From the darkness to the right, a faint sound of footfalls, light and swift, dwindled and vanished.

"She went this way!" the sorceress said. "Quickly!"

"No, wait!" Belgin barked. He stooped and examined the soft velvet of moss and mold coating the stone floor. "Aleena, bring your light here." The Waterdhavian stooped and spoke a word, brightening her wand. In the emerald light, Belgin traced a set of footprints. They initially turned toward the right but then doubled back in the other direction. The bard snorted in satisfaction. "She went left. I'm certain of it."

"What of the footfalls?" Miltiades said.

"A simple trick for any mage," Aleena replied. "Clearly, one of the personas she's absorbed was a skilled wizard. She can't be far. Good thinking, Belgin."

The sharper bowed with a smile. "Glad to have been of service, my lady."

Moving slowly now, the foursome advanced down the hallway to the left, alert for any sign of the doppelganger's presence. After sixty or seventy yards, the passage ended in a jagged tumble of stone and earth that completely blocked the corridor. There was no trace of Eidola.

"Perhaps she fooled us after all," Miltiades said in a tight voice. "Or fled through a secret passageway that we missed along the way."

"I don't think so," Belgin answered. "I've still got her track here. Either she passed through that—" he nodded at the cave-in—"or she's still here, hiding."

"We'll soon see," Aleena murmured. She uttered the words of a disenchantment, unbinding any spell within the vicinity. Silently, the four watched the end of the passageway.

Dust motes sparkled in the emerald light of Aleena's wand. Standing in front of the rockslide, a figure appeared suddenly from nothingness. As the spell of concealment failed, a handsome elven mage stood before them, glowering in anger. He started to raise his hands to work a spell, but Aleena pointed her wand at his midsection. "Don't even think about it," the Waterdhavian drawled.

"So. You have me cornered and outnumbered. What now?" the elf sneered. With a gesture of disdain, his features melted and reformed as the clear-eyed, strong visage of Eidola as they knew her. A keen short sword formed from one hand, and she crouched in a fencer's stance. "Will you destroy me with a slaying spell, then, Aleena? Smite me down with your hammer, Miltiades, after a noble challenge and trial by combat? How is it to be?"

"You will surrender," Miltiades stated clearly. "I intend to bring you back to answer for your crimes in person, Eidola. There's no easy way out of this for you."

Rings nudged Belgin. "The contract," he said quietly. "She dies here."

"Dissension among the ranks?" Eidola observed with a smile. "Kill me or capture me, which is it to be? Dear Miltiades, you won't allow these scoundrels to murder a prisoner under your protection, will you? Aleena, your father dies if the pirates strike me down."

Miltiades and Aleena glanced thoughtfully at the two Sharkers. "I cannot permit it, Belgin," the paladin said quietly.

Belgin looked from Eidola to Aleena to Rings. From his belt he drew Noph's lasso, looping it around his left wrist. Then he offered the end to Miltiades. As the paladin watched, he spoke. "I came here with the intention of killing her, and I am under a contract to do so. But here and now, I voluntarily break my contract with Entreri. I will not do his work here, not if the doppelganger can be taken alive and made to answer for what she's done." He looked down at his companion, and slipped the noose from his hand. "Rings?"

The dwarf scowled and swore but accepted the lariat. "I've never betrayed a contract in my life, but this one I'll break. I owe Artemis Entreri nothing. I agree with Belgin.

Take your prisoner, Miltiades."

The paladin retrieved Noph's lasso of truth from the dwarf's hand. "Thank you, Rings," he said. "I've had enough fighting to last me a lifetime." He turned and faced Eidola. "Now, for you. It's long past time that we heard you speak the truth, doppelganger."

"How charming," Eidola hissed. As Miltiades advanced on her, she suddenly pressed her fist into her midsection, just beneath her heart. Eyes dripping venom, she reached inside her own torso and removed a single white gemstone, holding it clenched in her hand. "Enough of this. Do any of you recognize what I hold in my hand?"

"A soul gem," Aleena gasped. "I thought as much!"

"Good," sneered Eidola. "Then you know that if I shatter it, that portion of your father's soul that I've trapped within is destroyed forever. Take another step, Miltiades, and I smash this thing. You'll bring me in to face your justice, but Piergeiron Paladinson will be condemned beyond any hope of resurrection. Do you understand me?"

"I understand," Miltiades answered gravely. The muscles of his jaw quivered with anger, but the noble paladin halted, watching the doppelganger. "Damn you, I understand."

"You will retreat down the hall and back up the stair you came down. Should I detect any sign that you are attempting to follow me again, I shall destroy the gem at once," Eidola said, smirking. "You've been an admirable foe, Miltiades, but I tire of this game." Holding the gem aloft, she advanced confidently, daring the paladin to interfere.

"Do not make the mistake of believing that I will allow you to leave, Eidola," Miltiades said evenly. He stood his ground, refusing to yield. "Damage that stone, and you will be dead before all the pieces hit the floor."

"I think not," Eidola snapped. "There's room for thousands of souls in this prison, paladin. Maybe it's time you became one of them!" She raised the soul gem high and started to shout an invocation or command, pointing at Miltiades with her free hand. The diamond began to glow with a pure white light. The paladin stood transfixed, gaping in horrified fascination at the approach of his doom.

Quick as thought, Belgin flipped a knife from his sleeve and threw it underhanded. The silver blade turned once before striking Eidola in her midriff. It was a small wound to the doppelganger, nothing more than a pinprick, but Eidola recoiled and gasped in pain, losing her spell. *"No!"* she shrieked.

In her hand, the soul gem blazed silently to an unbearable splendor. In one brilliant flash of supernal radiance, it seared the vision from Belgin's eyes and set him to blinking furiously. In his ears, Eidola's shriek of rage grew great and dark as a storm, surrounding him in spite and anger—and then it was gone.

When he could see again, Eidola stood still as a stone, her face frozen in a cold and fierce rage. She still held the soul gem clenched in her fist, but all color had been bleached from her body, leaving her white and pure as marble. Between her alabaster fingers, the diamond glittered coldly.

"Aleena? What happened?" whispered Miltiades.

Shaken, the Waterdhavian mage approached and peered into Eidola's contorted features. "I believe she trapped herself inside the gem," she said slowly. "I—I have seen this before. It's a devious device, and it can strike any who stand near when its power is invoked."

"Is she dead?" asked Rings.

"If only it were that simple," Aleena replied. Carefully, she reached out to open Eidola's hand and remove the stone, but the doppelganger's fingers refused to yield. "The soul gem destroys, yes, but in some way it also preserves what it takes in its crystalline depths. Eidola is somewhere within."

Miltiades bowed his head, wearied beyond human endurance. "Then our quest is at an end."

Postlude

Crystal and white surround me.

I am without form, without substance, a splinter in a sea of glass. I hear the others sometimes. They gibber and shriek; they moan and plead; a few seem to silently reflect and wait with a patience beyond my own. If I could find them, I would slay them for the peace they possess.

I've lost my others, my guises. They can't exist here, not in this realm of ultimate truth. How can a soul be something it is not? Here I am only the nameless mocker, the cold and vacant spirit that learned to walk in the shape of a man, an elf, a minotaur. My life was a mimicry, and without my others I have nothing left that is me.

There is one voice here I cannot bear. She's strong, and near to me, although I cannot see her. I want to kill her, to silence her reproach, but . . . I fear her. Here, she is greater than I could ever be. In this crucible of glass and light, I cannot exist. But she has endured here for time beyond measure. How long is a minute without a heartbeat to count it by? How long is a day without the sun? Yet she waits in this endless tedium, not content, and not afraid.

I can't bear the sound of her voice. She doesn't address me—no one here can know who or what they speak to. No one. It drives me to scream, to rage, to storm uselessly with all the fury at my command. In my darkness there is a scream that could shatter the world, if only I could give voice to it.

But she whispers of love.

The story continues . . .

THE DOUBLE DIAMOND TRIANGLE SAGA

The bride of the Open Lord of Waterdeep has been abducted. The kidnappers are from the far-off lands of the Utter East. But who are they? And what do they really want? Now a group of brave paladins must travel to the perilous kingdoms of this unknown land to find the answers. But in this mysterious world, nothing is ever quite what it appears.

Look for the complete collection of books

in the series

The Abduction
(January 1998)

The Paladins
(January 1998)

The Mercenaries
(January 1998)

Errand of Mercy
(February 1998)

An Opportunity for Profit
(March 1998)

Conspiracy
(April 1998)

Uneasy Alliances
(May 1998)

Easy Betrayals
(June 1998)

The Diamond
(July 1998)

Coming in July

THE DIAMOND

By J. Robert King & Ed Greenwood

The quest has taken two parties across the Realms. Now the heroes gather at Waterdeep, where it all began, for a final celebration. But there are still a few loose ends to tie up. . . .